AN ECLIPSE
OF
YESTERYEAR

DEEPAK RANJAN

NITESH KUMAR

First published in 2017 by

Becomeshakespeare.com
Wordit Content Design & Editing Services Pvt Ltd
Unit - 26, Building A-1, NrWadala RTO, Wadala (East),
Mumbai 400037, India
T:+91 8080226699

This book has been fully funded by the Wordit Art Fund.
Wordit Art Fund helps deserving authors publish their work by providing
monetary support. To apply for funding, please visit us at
www.BecomeShakespeare.com

©
ISBN: 978-93-86487-20-9

Cover Design ©Addictive Shots
Author Photography by Liptakant Mishra

Disclaimer
This is a work of fiction. Names, characters, businesses, places, events and
incidents are either the products of the author's imagination or used in a
fictitious manner. Any resemblance to actual persons, living or dead, or
actual events is purely coincidental.

DEDICATION

Deepak Ranjan
My Grandmother,
My first Storyteller, from whom listening stories, I grew up…

My Darling ANJALI & PAPA

Nitesh Kumar

My Mom & Dad who blessed me this life

My Sweet Sister & Brother who stand beside me

My Special Friend who has ever boosted me to achieve my goals &
dreams in life following the right path!

ACKNOWLEDGMENTS

We would like to express our heartfelt thanks:
- God, for HIS warm blessings and making me capable enough to pen my words on paper.
- My Grandparents, who were no more alive but their stories, affection and love is still alive in me. They were the one who inspired me with their story telling.
- My family, for their never-ending support and belief they have on me.
- Nitesh Kumar, my Co-Author, without whose effort the book would remain incomplete.
- My parents for their blessings to move ahead in the right path with intellectuality and wise thoughts.
- My family and friends who ever have supported me to achieve success.
- Sumit Mishra, the primary Editor of my book; whose untiring efforts made this book happens. Right from reading the draft full of errors to improvising it – his contribution is undoubtedly cherished and acknowledged.
- Achala Upendran for Editing, Proof-reading and ensuring the readability of the book.
- Our reviewers Poonam and Sonali, whose encouragement made us come up with this work...
- Our publishing Company Become Shakespeare and our publishing consultant Amrita Jagtap and team for providing us a platform to share our thoughts.
Last but not the least a big Thank you to all our wonderful readers out there. Your suggestions and feedback is highly appreciated!
We hope a long way to go with you people in future and hope you really enjoy reading our book. Thank you all once again...

CONTENTS

1. KILL HIM!

The stories of the era of mysticism that our grandparents spoke of told tales of kings, queens and other larger than life characters! The stories of magic, the stories of good versus evil, and love versus hatred, have a history of their own in our golden, magnanimous history. Whenever told, they make us believe in an unseen power, and we dream of living through the characters. The sunrise always comes after dusk; a great warrior is born from a bloody war and for a blessing to soothe a soul, it must have been tormented by a curse. 'The sky is vast, so is the world beneath. No power has been mighty enough to win all, and love can only win with submission first…' was the thought of one of the renowned warriors of that time, Flavius.

Being an obedient slave of Chief Mathews, he had devoted his life to expanding the empire by winning new territories for him. In him, people saw a great warrior with a great heart. He was a fatherly figure for the poor and a man who took care of the entire village. Chief Mathews had even promised to make Flavius' son the next Chief. But fate had its own plans for his son, who was born on the day of solar eclipse. Instead, the boy was a curse for the entire kingdom, as predicted by Guru Chandaliyan. The citizens' unquestioned obedience to the prophecies of Guru Chandaliyan brought Chief Mathews to crossroads, and he had to choose between common belief and the promise to his man.

Meanwhile, Flavius was no longer interested in fights in the arena, which had earned him the title of 'the Warrior Flavius.' He had made up his mind to leave them behind.

The roar of the crowd echoed throughout the arena. Some laughed, some whistled, and some clapped to encourage the fighters.

'Yeah… Do it…' the howling chorus was clearly audible.

'Oh Shit! Fuck Man…' Dejection descended on the crowd. The weak fighter was making it a difficult last fight for Flavius.

'Now for the final fight, our top two fighters stand in front of you, a big hand to both of them. Let's begin the most compelling show of this evening, with a big round of applause,' announced the confident trainer and commentator, Mercury.

'I bet everything I possess on this battle…' the red-masked Flavius took the vow, closing his eyes.

'For my child, my passion is the price I am ready to pay…' Flavius told the lady, tenderly holding her head in his hands.

'You mean no more fights after this…?' questioned a bewildered Alishan.

'I will not fight again if I win this! It has always been my intention to spend my last moments before fights with you, as they may well be the last moments of my life. Let's make these special, for they are going to be the last such before I finish fighting.'

'Nothing can stop you from returning to me, my love, my warrior. You will win. Tomorrow, with the sunrise, our love will bloom. One more achievement will be added to your glory. I believe in you,'

Alishan said, holding her husband close.

'My love, you should be brave to live with the truth; no one knows what life holds for us… It's not the opponent or the game, but fear of the dreadful possibility of not coming back to you that has been the most testing and trying part of my life. A warrior is not known by a name and face, but by the persona, he creates in battlefield. He cannot live to see his wife in the arms of his opponent, or his master! So, while handling over the weapon to the opponent after being defeated, his silence asks the warrior to spare him! If I lose the battle, I will lose everything…' Alishan put her hand on his lips, looking him into the eyes with love and assurance that he will be back.

Flavius was tall, but this was not a rarity among his people. While his round and wide shoulders made him appear stronger than most other warriors, his toned legs let him do most athletic exercises with ease. His sparkling eyes set under a broad forehead, emanated life and energy. A long and high nose and carved chin added to his features.

Flavius opened his eyes and raised his weapon to get the attention of the crowd. Then he started walking. Adjusting his red mask with his left hand, he raised his sword in the right, first pointing it towards the sky and then to the crowd. A resolute calmness glowed on his face. He growled a bit and paced towards his opponent who had put on his black mask and begun his move.

The crowd was cheering, 'Go on Flavius… Satrugna!!! Slay him.' Both warriors were rushing towards each other now, fire in their eyes, concentrating on each other. As they came closer, Flavius struck first. Satrugna defended. As their swords clashed, the crowd's roaring was dwarfed by that of the weapons. Flavius's rapid and resolute strikes kept black-masked Satrugna defending himself. The fight was between equals as the division of the cheering crowd signified.

Suddenly, Satrugna stopped defending, and held Flavius by his wrists, blocking his powerful, ferocious attacks. Both warriors were grunting, facing each other, circling in the arena. Flavius tried to free his hands from his opponent's grip, but he couldn't. He stepped back, raised his leg and kicked Satrugna's chest with great force. Satrugna stepped back and managed not to tumble over. He controlled himself and attacked Flavius without any break. It seemed impossible for him to defeat Flavius, so he came closer and walloped Flavius from the back with his elbow. Flavius grew furious and moved his sword, which left a cut on Satrugna's shoulder. The cut started bleeding profusely, and a feeble moan could be heard. As he turned back, Flavius attacked again. With the deep cut on his back, Satrugnacouldn't hold the sword tight, and at another blow, it slipped out of his hands. Now Satrugna was without any weapon. Flavius left deep cuts on his arms with frequent attacks. Another on his thighs! The deep cuts were bleeding badly.

'Flavius, show the crowd that you are more than a man! A legend of our generation! Show your hunger to win, your thirst to drink the blood of the fucking shit in front of you'!' Elvin, Flavius's close friend shouted.

Both warriors, fighting for 'everything or nothing,' were not ready to lose an inch without giving up blood.

All eyes were focused on the center of the arena and the crowd was waiting to see one man emerge as a winner. Flavius was moving very fast, and so was his weapon. In the background, the crowd parted in two, splitting into the supporters of Flavius and Satrugna.

'Attack…' a roar repeatedly rose from the crowd.

And finally, Flavius seized his moment. Satrugna was off balance, thanks to the cut on his leg. He fell on the sand. Flavius lost no time in putting his weapon to the neck of the fallen man, and his other leg on his chest. Chief Mathews seemed to be perplexed, watching the game.

'Kill him! Separate his head from his body, C'mon...!' the crowd bellowed. With pride, Flavius looked up to the sky. Just then, a weak grip on his leg and the pleading words of a woman forced him to look down. The cry of the woman made him a bit nervous, and he took his foot away from Satrugna's chest. It was a dilemma for Flavius now, whether to listen to his conscience or to follow the rules of the game. The rules dictated that he kill Satrugna. As customary, victory had tobe marked by the red blood of the defeated, and all belongings of the vanquished would be transferred to the winner.

'Whenever there is confusion between your mind and conscience, listen to your conscience ...' Alishan's words echoed in his ears, and for few moments he was standing still with an unclear mind, his stressed face reflected the confusion inside. Just then, he felt the sharpness of a weapon at his neck. When he tried to turn back, Satrugna moved his sword very fast with all his might. In no time, he was soaked in red. The woman ran away frightened, splashes of blood on her face. The supporters of Satrugna started cheering: 'Kill him..., kill him...'

Elvin closed his eyes. But Flavius stood up with the support of his sword, and lunged with all the energy he had left. Satrugna was now cleverly hitting at his cuts and wounds to make Flavius scream in pain. Flavius kicked him hard, and Satrugna moved behind, then jumped over Flavius, trying to make him fall on the ground. A sudden jerk from the back pulled Flavius' mask off. Before he could gather his senses, Satrugna had put his leg on his chest and stabbed him in the chest.

'My friend, it's our pride that helps us grow. And as a warrior, I want to leave this earth, not as the vanquished but the vanquisher...' Flavius's words echoed in the ears of Elvin, who was crying, seeing

Flavius lying in a pool of blood.

'I won't decapitate you, since you spared my life,' Satrugna whispered, looking at him.

An unnatural storm descended, the wind blowing thick with sand. The sun was setting behind the mountains, lighting up a red sky. The birds were flying back to their nests, marking the end of their struggle. The time had arrived to take rest, the end of a day.

2. THE WILD CAT

'Please spare him! Have mercy on him! He is innocent.'

A woman was begging for someone's life. But the mob was marching on, passing all the stones and broken trees in the dark.

The crowd shouted 'Don't leave them… Smash them.'

A woman could be seen moving quickly in the dark forest. It was pitch dark with stars fighting to be visible in the absence of the moon.

The mob carried axes, swords, and sticks which were partly visible in the yellow light of the torch. Suddenly they stopped running, and there came a furious question from the leader, Elvin.

'Where has she gone? She must be hiding somewhere. We have to search and find her. We must kill her baby. We will slay them.'

At the top of the tree under which the men were panting, an owl started hooting in a very unusual manner. The men looked up and tried to scare the owl, but it wouldn't stop. The man carrying the lamp dropped it in tension and fear. The lamp went out.

All the others laughed at him.

'I think we should go back to the village,' he said.

'Are you scared?'

'Yes…given the night and the place and situation we are in, I am not ashamed to say that I am.'

Far away to the north, a pack of wolves was howling.

'Our lamp has been extinguished. I think we should go back to the village.'

'Shut your mouth. If you want to go back, you may, but we will return only after killing the child,' said Elvin.

Everyone's eyes were pulled by a movement in the bush. 'There she is…' one of them whispered.

'Give me the baby, Alishan. It's me, Elvin. I respect the mother in you, but it's a curse. Please try to understand. We have lost a great warrior because of this demon!'

Suddenly the moon peeped out from behind the clouds.

There was movement behind the bushes, again. The men were almost upon her. The woman was sweating, and trying to cover whatever she held in the veil of her thin saree.

'Just be careful, and move straight. We're closing on her…'

Now they were closer, and they raised their axes, the swords and the sticks.

All the men were anxious and alert, their hearts pounding. As they raised their weapons higher, the man who had carried the lamp spoke, 'Wait, look over there.'

Everyone looked. They saw a stone, two green flares above it glowing in the dark, slowly moving. There came a low pitched growl.

Suddenly the clouds parted, and they could see.

At the sight, the men dropped their weapons, terrified. A wild cat was facing them, its eyes alight with rage.

The woman was terrified by the sight. A baby started crying, roused by the loud growl. The wild cat moved its eyes towards the lady and growled again, drowning out the baby's cry.

One of the men whispered, 'Be alert and calm everyone. Don't you even think of picking up the weapons! Your movement may annoy the wild cat.'

The animal moved slowly towards the lady. The woman kept her eyes fixed on the cat.

As the cat ran, Elvin said, 'Now it's moving towards the curse, and it will kill him and maybe the mother as well. As it moves towards them, we should step back, but slowly! Raghu, you move first.'

Raghu, the man who had held the lamp, stepped back. As his foot landed on dried leaves, the sound drew the attention of the wild cat. Its eyes followed the sound and it started growling again. As the others started moving back, the ferocious animal's thunder began to echo throughout the dark forest. And, then it turned towards the group. One of the men hurriedly ran away, leaving the others, and the cat jumped on him.

The man was screaming and shivering in fear. The cat put its paw on his chest and started swinging its tail and growled, as if this was the end. Another man from the group gathered his courage and yelled at his friend to stay still.

Stoned with fear, the man lay still on the ground. The tiger left him. As he started crawling back and got up hurriedly, the tiger finally caught hold of his neck. He screamed, and the silence of the forest was broken by despair.

Alas, when his life ebbed and the cries for help fell silent, the wolves began howling. The tiger's eyes were burning and it licked its nose. It growled but now at a lower pitch. When it had turned its back on the group, one of the men bent down to pick up a weapon. He managed to grab a stick. As he was about to rise with the stick, another jump from the tiger sent the stick flying and the man stumbling to the ground. Bleeding and crying, he died.

Swinging its tail, it turned back. The remainder of the mob was sure of their imminent deaths, and decided to fight rather than die screaming. Thinking this, all the men picked up their arms as fast as they could. The tiger, irritated by this arrogance, roared ferociously.

The lady was terrified seeing the dead man in front of her. Blood was still dripping from the stone on which the body lay lifeless. She felt the same blood on her face. She tried to move, but she lost her senses and fell unconscious.

The baby was crying louder than ever. Though unconscious, her grip on the child was firm. The incessant movements of the baby caused the *saree* of the unconscious lady to slip off, leaving her breast bare. The baby seemed hungry but being unconscious, the mother was not in a position to suckle him. Though the kid tried, he was not strong enough to bring his mouth to the nipple.

The sky could not stand by as a dumb spectator, and it started thundering with anger, the wind started blowing. Rain began to fall, as if hurt by the lady's helplessness; and the heavenly bodies seemed about to drown the world in tears.

A woman feels safe in any situation and any part of the world when her man stands beside her. But this was a dreadful moment of Alishan's life. She was unable to protect the precious life in her hands

17

though she wanted to. She was all alone, unconscious, and barely covered in torn clothes. Alishan had never been in such a helpless condition before.

Now the wild cat was surrounded by four men, armed with various weapons. Meanwhile, sensing the situation, the tiger became more aggressive. The war was getting more intense without any actual attack from either side. Any wrong move from either side would be decisive.

Though the men had the advantage of numbers, nature favoured the beast. On the one hand was a born hunter, while on the others were merely trained warriors already in shock at having lost two of their comrades. The tiger had its bodily arms of nails and teeth, whereas the men held weapons. The beast lived in and ruled the forest. On the other hand, the men were in unfamiliar territory. A human can try and become wild, but becoming ferocious at will is in the animals' nature.

Moving swiftly, the tiger added two more men to its total. The remaining four were now sweating, numb, the objective of killing the cursed child having long left their minds. The instinct of survival dominated all their thoughts and actions. Everyone was on high alert.

The tiger shook its body, starting from its nose to its tail tip, seeking to dry itself. The men seized this advantage, and three of them stepped forward raising their weapons, but the fourth one lagged behind. As they stepped ahead, the tiger grabbed the fourth one with just one jump, and the game was over for him. Seeing this, the other three raised their axes and ran towards the beast. The tiger turned back, raised its upper legs and widened its mouth. The growling scared the men off. They went numb and were unable to move their hands. The tiger in the meantime opened its claws and pounced directly on the second person's bare neck and then jumped on the other one without any delay. This time, the nails pierced in the third man's chest and with a thud he fell down with the tiger on top of him.

The last man standing was Elvin. Though the strongest of the group, he was dumbstruck by seeing his fellow men dying like puppets against the mighty tiger. He stepped back with his hands up in the air and his eyes on the wild beast. Elvin gathered all the courage and energy left in him to overcome fear and despair. As he moved forward to surprise the big cat, he was surprised to find his left leg strangled by roots, pulling him down to the ground. He fell on his chest; his head struck the trunk of a tree. The tiger moved to him, smelled him, and moved his face with its paws. There was no reaction.

It turned away and raised itself on the stone, roaring into the jungle and rain.

In the heavy rain, a few big branches broke from the tree and fell to the ground, shaking the ground and the bushes, and sprinkling some water on the unconscious Alishan.

The tiger moved to the crying baby and took a close look of him. The innocent child touched the tiger's nose, which tickled the tiger and it growled. As Alishan slowly opened her eyes, she saw the blood-soaked face of the beast near her baby. With a shout, she dragged her baby close to her bare chest, trying to hide it from the beast. The tiger responded to that cry with a growl, stepped back and sat on the stone again.

The rain stopped after some time. The tiger began cleaning itself. The baby started suckling with some help from the mother. Everything submitted to the calm and the stillness that prevailed after the storm. But so many things had already changed.

Alishan was bewildered and confused at still being alive. The death of

Flavius and the turn of events in her life seemed part of a distant past.

After the baby's hunger has been quenched, he slept. ButAlishan didn't move her eyes from the tiger looking at her child.

The beast got up, shook its body and jumped down from the stone. Alishan hugged the child more closely. The tiger just looked at her once, growled softly and disappeared in the dark.

Alishan took in a long breath. She held up her baby and kissed it all over. Then she looked up into the sky and thanked the gods. She searched for a safe space to hide. There was an opening in the high grounds, which appeared to be the entry to a dark cave. She sniffed the air, looking for the scent of a beast, but the air smelled pleasant. Finally, she curled up inside, and lost herself to sleep.

3. THE SWEET MOAN

Chief Mathews was sitting on a throne flanked by two kinsmen. He was smoking the *hookah*. A twin to his chair stood beside him, vacant. Some men were squatting on the floor in front of him.

An old man carrying a bunch of registers came forward. 'Chief; I have checked these records, but…'

Mathews raised his hand. The old man shut his mouth.

'Look who is here! The great one among warriors! Welcome! Who is she? Did you get married?'

'Yes, Master. I got married in the temple and have come here to seek your blessings.'

The young warrior Flavius and his wife came up the stairs. The men squatting on the ground moved aside, making way. The Chief was blushing and curling his moustache tips with his fingertips. As the couple came near the chair, they bent down, put their heads to his bare feet in submission. The Chief leant forward and blessed them.

'May you both prosper in life and stay happily together for a lifetime. Get up…'

He helped them up.

'You're a lucky one,' he said to Flavius. 'Your lady is a masterpiece of beauty.'

'Thank you, Master.'

Tapping the woman's shoulder, the Chief asked, 'Your name?'

'Alishan,' replied Flavius, speaking for his shy wife.

'Oh... Alishan... Let's take a walk,' the chief said.

The woman raised her lowered eyes. 'Where?'

'To the temple with Master. It's our tradition. Go...' Flavius explained.

Alishan held her man's hand, requesting he accompany them. But Flavius freed his hand and said, 'Not me, only you! Follow the Master.'

The Master moved ahead, into the interiors of his palace. The young Alishan looked at her husband with an expression he could not decipher as she followed. She kept turning back to look at him, as though hoping he would follow.

The Chief lit an oil lamp and offered it to the deity in the temple. He murmured a few *shlokas* and offered some flowers. He motioned to Alishan, who was standing behind him, to do the same.

While offering the flowers, he supported the woman's hands from below. His eyes were dancing with joy as she closed her eyes. Mathews took pleasure in staring at Alishan's body. His imagination went wild, and he yearned to unravel her *saree*.

Alishan opened her eyes and sprinkled the flowers on the idol of the deity. She folded her hands. The Master took some vermillion in his fingers and tried to put it on the lady's head, but she resisted by moving a step back.

'This is god's blessing; there is nothing to fear dear. It doesn't matter who puts it on your head...' the Chief said, trying to soothe her.

The lady reluctantly agreed. She put it on and then picked up a plate and made some offerings to the deity.

Alishan raised her eyes and looked into those of the Chief. They were sparkling with evil intent.

She took some *prasad* from the plate held by Mathews and put it in her mouth. It tasted different from regular *Prasad,* but before she could think of why, she lost her senses, and the Chief caught her in his arms.

Greedily, he hugged Alishan to his chest. Holding her, he began kissing her forehead, cheeks, nose, lips and behind her ears. He even started licking the lady's face with his tongue, tasting her salty sweat. He then carried her to a room.

After laying her body on a bed, he started kissing her greedily all over her body. Now before the final act, he stood up. He went to the side of the bed, lifted up a jug and glass, poured wine into the glass and drank it down. After four to five glasses of the drink, he was high. Everything seemed to be revolving, and the lady seemed to be calling to him. He poured more wine into the glass and moved forward, but his legs got stuck in the table legs and the wine spilt from his glass on the lady's face. Some went inside her nostrils and choked her. She started coughing and slowly opened her eyes. She sat up holding her head in pain and as she regained her consciousness, she was shocked to find herself in bed, her dress dishevelled. While getting up from the bed and setting her *saree* right, her eyes surveyed the room. After some time, she found the intoxicated Chief fallen on the floor with his head on the edge of the bed.

Her eyes became moist and tears rolled down her cheeks. She started running towards the door, wiping her face. But, suddenly an old lady appeared in front of her, and she stopped.

'Dear, don't fear… nothing has happened to you!'

The old lady understood the question in Alishan's eyes and answered with an unbelievable composure.

'I'm a servant, and have worked in this palace for the last fifty years. I know everything about Mathews, his character and his family! But as I'm only a servant, I've no option but to obey. When a newlywed couple comes to him, he holds the newlywed wife for the first night. The speaking mouth and the listening ear don't pose any threat to the Chief's secret. He drugs the *prasad*, and when the lady falls unconscious after eating it, he destroys her virginity.'

'What if I tell my husband? He is a great warrior; he is undefeated. He will punish him,' Alishan said.

'No one has ever dared to raise eyes to this family and neither will your husband. He is bound to remain silent. If not, he will be dead and so will you, so better you never discuss this with your husband or any other person. That's my advice,' the old lady insisted.

She continued, 'Leave this cruel instance behind you, and enjoy your new life. Forget about this. No one will point finger at you.'

Alishan thanked the woman and moved ahead, wiping her tears and giving a fake smile on approaching her husband.

Flavius held his beautiful wife's hand and walked outside.

24

A dark room lit by an oil lamp. A newlywed bride sitting with her head between her knees, sobbing.

The creaky door opened and the warrior entered with a red rose in his hands. He sat on the bed beside her, and raised his bride's face to his, but it was not visible in the dark. He turned up the flame of the lamp.

'It is as if the moon has come into my room, tearing the darkness. As if the lotus has blossomed from the mud. You've lifted up my life, my love! These tears rolling down your cheeks are like diamonds which are very precious, so don't let them fall. Otherwise the burglars might steal them away.' The woman smiled at the poetry.

'Even your smiling teeth look like precious stones! Now, a small beauty for the most beautiful lady in the world.' He handed over the red rose.

Alishan took it in her right hand, and Flavius pulled the left towards himself and kissed it. She turned her face to his. Now he leant forward, Alishan lowered her eyes and twisted her lips. He took off her nose ring. Then both earrings, one by one, then pulled at the *pallu* covering her bosom. Shyly, she moved off the bed and stood on the floor with her face turned towards the wall.

'All my life, I have tasted only blood in battles. For the first time, I am going to feel love. My lady from my dreams!'

Flavius got off the bed, went towards her, kissed her back and neck, and loosened the ties of her blouse. He held her tightly around her waist.

This kiss below her ears aroused her passion. She turned her face towards her man and hugged him. He passionately kissed her lips. With one hand on her breast, he used the other to loosen her petticoat, watched it fall. He stepped back, and kissed her bared bosom. He removed her bangles to mute all the other sounds apart from the music of their passionate breaths. Then he kissed her again. They closed their eyes. The hug was getting tighter and tighter. The lady's breath grew faster and faster, and her nails pierced his back. But there was no pain, only love; passionate love prevailed.

Flavius lifted Alishan and moved her to the bed. Removing his under clothes, he laid his bare body on the lady's tender one, and turned off the oil lamp.

Alishan moaned a little as the two became one. Only the sounds of young love were audible in the dark until the sun rose, letting its rays tear the darkness and enter the room. Along with the light, screeching birds, the crowing cocks joined the romantic tune of the love birds.

When light entered the room, it found them both on the bed, the man up on the lady and moving up and down. The woman felt every pump with great love. Finally, at the climax, he released all his love inside the woman, and exhausted, fell upon her with closed eyes. The woman began licking and biting her man's face. He lifted his head and kissed her lips.

'Are you alright my love? Did I hurt you? Are you satisfied?'

'It was painful. Still, I saw heaven while making love to you. You've completed me. You are special to me. But how did you resist so long…, making love!' Alishan asked.

'I heard your sweet moan, while I was inside you… I desired to listen more, and this desire to hear you more and more, held me to act accordingly.'

4. BIRTH OF THE CURSE!

'My love, you deserve this. I'm a warrior who has defeated many strong men in the field. How can I accept defeat so early?'

'So you won tonight.'

'No, my love, I'm defeated by your love…!'

The lady locked lips with him again.

With time, their bonds grew stronger. Their love multiplied day by day. She loved the tender heart the ferocious warrior nested in his chest. On the day of a fight, Alishan always prepared the pooja thali with an oil lamp, said her prayers and put vermillion on his forehead, wishing him good luck. She would hand over the sword herself and wish him victory. Flavius would walk out and then suddenly return, lift up his lady and kiss her mischievously. This was part of their routine.

Even Alishan's cooking was splendid. If Flavius was present, he disturbed her, with a little tickle here or there or else by planting a soft kiss on her neck or shoulder, whatever appealed to him at that moment. He stopped only when his mother interrupted them with her coughing from the other room. His mother also was euphoric, seeing both of them happy.

Flavius practised with his sword every day in the backyard, and whenever Alishan visited him, he would hand the sword over to her.

'I don't like violence. I can't handle it.'

'Being my wife, you should not fear this. You must know this art. It will be helpful to you when I'm not with you.'

Though he used fear to motivate her, he despised the idea of such a future, praying that the day would never come, that Alishan would never have to face the world on her own. Her training began.

Alishan loved sitting near the shore, but Flavius never had any interest in it. Still, whenever Alishan demanded Flavius's presence, he would accompany her. They would walk to the top of the big rock, on the beach. Flavius would carry her on his back, and seat beside him. Alishan rested her head on his shoulder and sometimes on his lap. She would tell tales of their future, and Flavius used to listen as though planning to make all those dreams real. There was no time-limit; sometimes they would sit fort the whole day and sometimes the whole night!

The only constant in life is change. The waves form, traverse the water, making it arduous for the swimmer, but even those mighty waves die at the seashore.

The story of life goes on, and the romance of life is never-ending! The dreams, and secrets whispered between lovers are things that add colour to life. They don't know what to say for so long, what stories to whisper. But when they leave the whole world and sit in seclusion in their own, they don't know how they lose control over words. It always seems to be something new, listening to dreams, most of which can lose sense for them if try to understand them closely. Such was their condition.

Once one starts listening, s/he becomes just a listener, and the partner becomes the best storyteller. For them, the characters in their stories live more than any living being in reality.

When Flavius would open his eyes, he would see the multi-coloured sky, as if an artist had painted the big canvas, pulling it towards the end of the day.

'I can't believe the day has gone, and it's dusk now...'

The storyteller and the listener would be hidden from each other at that time. But still, the voice and the beautiful words would remain in the air.

'I want to listen longer... I want to hear it all. Tell me a new story to the next twilight, my love. Please don't stop.'

Time was flying, but not the charm and freshness of their love.

One day, Alishan felt nauseous while serving dinner. She ran outside. Flavius got up and followed her. She vomited, and Flavius grew nervous. 'Are you alright? What's the matter? Shall we go to the Vaidya?'

Alishan washed her face, put his hand on her belly and whispered in his ear, 'Your love has started growing in me.'

Flavius started caring more for his love. He showered love on his lady as her physical appearance began to change.

29

On hearing the news of her pregnancy, Alishan's father Syombhu Murthy visited her.

The day of pain came. A few women hovered around her, carrying vessels of hot water, others bore torn clothes, and covered Alishan where she lay on a bed. One senior and very experienced old lady (the daaimaa) was in charge of the whole procedure. Alishan was crying in pain while the other women held her tightly to stabilise her.

The new life was about to come. Dipping the torn clothes in hot water, the women placed them over the womb to pressurise it. Alishan was squealing continuously.

Finally! The baby came out drenched in blood. After cutting the cord, *daaimaa* lifted the child and pinched his butt. He cried. Everyone congratulated each other, and one of the women went out to announce to the waiting people: 'Congratulations. It's a baby boy.'

Flavius knelt down, crying with joy. Overwhelmed, he was babbling, 'Is my wife alright? And the baby…is the baby alright? Can we see them? Can I see them?'

'Have patience. Both the mother and child are fine. Yes, of course, you can meet them, but not before giving us our reward and gifts.'

'Of course! You have given me the most precious news in the world. I will not let you down. But let me have a look please,' he said and went in with anxiety.

The baby was getting breastfed. Flavius stood over his wife, looking at both of them without saying a word. His eyes became moist and tears rolled down his cheeks. Elvin and Alishan's father entered. Alishan covered her breasts and the baby with her clothes.

'I've become a father. This is one of the most memorable and happiest days of my life,' Flavius said.

In the outer room, people gathered to greet and welcome a new life into the world.

'I heard a boy has taken birth in the warrior's house,' a rough voice said.

'Yes, my lord,' Flavius's mother replied. She allowed the man to come inside.

As he entered, Flavius went down on his knees and bent his head. 'Hail, my Lord. Your blessings have brought me a baby boy.'

'He is a curse. You have to end this, warrior, or else it will be the reason for your end,' the man said very arrogantly.

5. CHANDALIYAN'S PREDICTION

'Lord, pardon me. I don't understand.'

'This child has been born on the day of an atrocious omen.'

The man in saffron clothes turned around and went outside. With a perplexed look in her eyes, Alishan looked up at her man. Flavius looked away from his lady, dazed, his eyes seeking to follow the man outside. His father-in-law and Elvin followed him.

He found the man sitting under a banyan tree, surrounded by villagers. Flavius rushed towards him and knelt before him.

'Lord… what's the matter? I am unable to figure it out, please help me,' he pleaded.

The man spoke in a commanding voice. 'Today is the day of evil. Evil becomes potent and rules over the divine. Today is the day of the solar eclipse. The Sun, despite being the dominant element of the world, gets defeated by the devil on this day and any child who is born on this day will be a devil's son. He is a danger to the beautiful world we live in. According to my calculations, this child was born at the very moment the devils were at their peak. The child is your son.'

There was dead silence. The villagers looked at each other with sorrow and pity for Flavius in their eyes.

Flavius's father-in-law asked very politely, 'My Lord! Is there any way to reverse the spell?'

'There is only one way out. Kill it!' the man commanded.

'No!' yelled Flavius. He's just a baby. I don't see how he can be of any danger to the world!'

'Have mercy on him. I promise and assure everyone that I will never let him go down the wrong path. I'll guide him every single moment. Please!'

'You're not the warrior I have known. I feel this child has taken over your senses!' exclaimed the man. 'You don't have any idea how destructive he can be, not only to others, but also to you and your family. This is not my opinion, it is my prediction. Has my prediction ever gone wrong?'

The villagers shouted 'No!'

The man was a preacher, a public figure respected by the village for his predictions. He was known as Swami Chandaliyan, the great lord of the village.

Some years earlier...

'Lord, my husband has not spoken for a whole week. He was checked by Sailya Vaidya, but today he was declared dead. Please do something for the sake of the child in my womb.'

'He will see your child for sure. I won't let it happen otherwise.'

'Lord, please show some mercy to us. It's my fault that I thought of taking him to Vaidya. This is the result of my ignorance,' the lady cried out loud.

'Come with me…'

All the villagers followed Chandaliyan to the graveyard.

The old guard of the cemetery was ready to set fire to the dead body. When he heard the sound of people approaching, he stopped. He stepped back with the torch in his hand.

Chandaliyan closed his eyes, everyone's focus shifted from the body to him. The lady stood still with her hands folded, hoping for the best.

Chandaliyan started walking around the body. As he walked, villagers saw a circle of fire forming a boundary around the corpse. As he walked, the guard felt uncomfortable and seemed to be choking. In no time, he had vanished. Chandaliyan completed twenty-one rounds of the body before he stopped. Only he knew that the guard who had disappeared had died on his way home.

'It happens! Someone has to pay for it and maybe that someone is you!' Chandaliyan whispered to the air.

The clouds started thundering, bringing rain and extinguishing the fire. The villagers chanted mantras with Chandaliyan, but suddenly he stopped the recitation.

'Lady, your husband is now breathing. You can check.'

The lady ran towards her husband to check if he was breathing.

'Don't worry, he'll be back on his feet soon,' continued Chandaliyan.

The woman touched his feet and started crying in happiness.

'May God bless you, my child,' he said.

The villagers were astonished at seeing this miracle performed in front of their eyes. They started cheering Chandaliyan as he left the premises.

These were some of the stories that had made Chandaliyan the living god of the village. People trust him blindly. All the married women would come to him for blessings and the poor would come to him for good fortune. There had been many incidents that proved his superiority; many women who had been unable to bear children were able to conceive after receiving his blessings. Everyone believed Chandaliyan had a solution to their miseries.

It was a common belief that if he wished, the sun wouldn't show its face. Once upon a time, farmers had lost their livelihoods because of drought and Chandaliyan with his power brought an ample amount of rain for the crops throughout the month. It was also believed that he could change the gender of a child if he wished and could also control disturbed and mad horses.

Chandaliyan opened his eyes and started screaming in anger.

'I can see the future. This child will bring catastrophe with his destructive powers and within ten days, the village is going to be ruined. The first one to burn in the fire of approaching death will be his father.'

'My Lord, is there any way out rather than killing?' asked the villagers, with a concern for the warrior who had been very generous and kind to everyone.

Chandaliyan closed his eyes again and chanted. Then he declared, 'Hand the child over to me and forget him. With my magical power, I will control him and his evil powers. He will stay with me at my residence. No one will see him.'

35

'Please, my Lord… figure some other way out. We'll die without him!' cried Flavius.

'You will die sooner or later! This is the truth. You can only buy some time.'

'We can't leave him. I choose to die for my baby. But I won't give him to someone else.'

'Try to understand,' the villagers spoke up. 'You can't put our lives at stake because of your love for a devil! This village is also yours, and we are your people.'

Syombhu said, 'Wait, let's see what happens. The prediction may go wrong. Let's wait for some days to see the truth.'

'The Lord's prediction can never go wrong and has never gone wrong,' the villagers said.

'Please, if not for the baby, at least for the sake of a man who has just received the happiness of being a father, who has always helped everyone, and stood beside you in your troubles; at least for his sake… We should wait and watch. Then, if things go wrong as per the prediction, we can move ahead. No one will stop you,' Elvin said.

'If you are willing to take the risk of challenging my prediction then do so, but I must say you will regret it.' Saying this, Chandaliyan left.

'Hold on, my friend. We are with you. Don't worry. Nothing will go wrong, believe me,' Elvin said, consoling the warrior. Syombhu nodded in hope and support.

'No. This can't be true. My child is not a curse; it is my love. Our love! Promise me you will never change your decision, no matter

36

what may come.' Alishan spoke in a hurried voice, holding the baby and pressing it close to her heart.

'I promise,' Flavius said in a shaky voice.

They both sat there, the baby in her arms, cursing their life as the day passed. With their eyes glazed, they lay down beside each other. Flavius blew the lamp out and kissed her lady's forehead as they closed their eyes.

Alishan woke with a shock, startled by the sounds of people protesting. She patted her husband's shoulder, trying to make him conscious of the sound. When he got up, the chorus of the crowd was audible to him, and in no time, the grumbling was even more distinguishable. Alishan was staring at him with a question in her eyes. Flavius hurriedly ran out of his house with a sword. As soon as he stepped out, he saw his house had been surrounded by villagers. Elvin was also surprised at seeing the crowd in front of the house.

'What's the matter?' Flavius asked.

'The tiger in the jungle attacked four men and killed three of them. The last one was lucky enough to run for life but still received a deadly injury. The prediction is coming true and one day it will ruin our village! Everything is going to be destroyed! All this happened because of that evil child!' a man blabbered.

'Shut your mouth. The tiger has attacked our village many times before. How is this related to the prediction?' Elvin asked.

'More than one person has never lost life to the tiger. Is this not the start of destruction?'

'Flavius, you should go back inside. Stay with your child, I'll manage this!' Elvin insisted.

Flavius retreated, shutting the front door.

Every passing day, mishaps were reported in the village and assumed to be connected to the prophecy. Soon enough, the supporters of the prediction started increasing in number but still no one had the guts to stand against a warrior as strong as Flavius.

Alishan was resting near her husband.

'For my child, my passion is a small fee I am ready to pay,' Flavius told her, tenderly holding her head in his hands.

'God! You mean no more fights after this?' asked the bewildered Alishan.

'Not a fight again if I win this! As it has always been my habit to spend my last moment with you before a fight, let's make this one special, for it is the last time.'

'Nothing can stop you from returning to me, my love, my warrior. You will win. Tomorrow, with the sunrise, our love is expected to bloom. One more achievement will be added to your glory. I believe in you.'

Both souls could have shed flesh if possible, the only cloth worn at that time. Alishan was resting in the arms of Flavius. Flavius kissed her neck and then moved his lips to kiss hers, very passionately.

'My love, you should be brave to live with the truth; no one knows what life holds for us... It's not the opponent or the game, but fear of the dreadful possibility of not coming back to you that has been the most testing and trying part of my life. A warrior is not known by a name and face, but by the persona that he creates in battle. He cannot live to see his wife in the arms of his opponent, or his master! So, while submitting the weapon, his silence asks the opponent to spare him! If I lose the battle, I will lose everything.'

Alishan put her hand over his lips, cutting him short.

On the morning of the last fight, Alishan helped Flavius with his bath. And then Flavius pulled her as well. They lived every moment of their life loving each other. She got him ready for the day. There was fear in her eyes, and so they grew moist with tears.

'Don't be so weak my love. I will be there for you and our child, all the time. No one will ever dare to touch him. It's time to go for the game. Another victory is waiting for me.' He kissed her forehead. 'And if something happens to me, then I've shared my art with you. It will protect you, if not me! Strengthen yourself and let me go, my love.'

The lady wiped her face and turned around. She brought the *pooja thali*, lit the lamp. Holding the child in one arm, she came to the warrior, handed over the *thali* and turned around to bring the sword. She put vermillion on his forehead and on his sword, threw flowers on him and finally lit the lamp and wished him good luck and victory.

The warrior kissed her on lips as if it were the last kiss and then he kissed his baby. His eyes were moist.

'I promise, my love, this is the last fight. After my victory, we will leave this village with our child and move far away, where no one would be able to trace our identity. We will prove the prediction wrong, our child is not evil. He was born of our love. I promise this.'

39

He turned around to leave the room. His mother was waiting at the door in the other room with the kavach, which she put on his neck and tied it around his chest. Her eyes were wet. The warrior touched her feet, kneeling down to seek her blessings.

6. FLAVIOUS'S LAST FIGHT

'Go ahead! Victory will be yours. Defeat whosoever comes in front of you and bring back glory with your name. Promise me you won't disappoint me.'

'I promise, Maa,' he said, and left with his dearest friend Elvin, who was waiting for him at the entrance. He didn't turn to look back as that would have made him appear weak. Both ladies stood there watching him leave with tears in their eyes and didn't move until he was out of sight.

Alishan was breastfeeding her baby. She was tense thinking about the future of her family. Suddenly, the loud sound of something breaking shocked her.

Anxiously, Alishan got up, holding the baby in her arms. She went outside and saw a man standing in front of her mother-in-law. On the ground was broken water pot with water spilt all over the floor.

Seeing the tears in her mother in law's eyes, Alishan was worried. 'What's the matter?' she asked.

41

When she didn't receive a response, Alishan got worried and shook her shoulders. This time, the old lady turned towards her and her lips quivered. She pushed her hands off her shoulder. Now the old woman's eyes were burning in anger, seeing the baby and the mother holding him. Tears were unstoppable for both ladies.

The man spoke out, breaking the silence. 'We should make a move before they come after us.'

The old lady squealed in despair, 'My son!' and ran from the house, followed by the man. Alishan yelled out, 'No... it mayn't happen! My heart knows he is fine!' and followed the old lady.

All of them rushed into the forest. It was getting dusky; the birds were returning from their long search for food. In the middle of the woods, they had to cross a canal via a wooden bridge. But due to their fast movements, the bridge's panels grew weaker, and as soon as Alishan stepped over them with her baby, they broke. She was hanging from the bridge, one leg stuck between the panels. This caused unbearable pain. She struggled but was unable to get loose. She yelled out for help, but no one came. The helpless woman was struggling alone with a baby in her arms. It was getting darker. Even the water of the canal was drifting at even faster pace, and if by chance the old bridge collapsed, then she would have lost her life to the alligators waiting for their feast below. Carefully holding the baby, she struggled to move the side panels with her other arm. She then placed her free leg firmly on the other panel which was intact, and tilting her body to the left, she put the ankle on the plank. Finally, she pulled herself up and came out. Once she had loosened herself, she carefully crossed the bridge and started running, following the path.

Flavius's body was not strong enough to attack and defeat his opponent. He raised his sword, but the opponent stopped the stroke with his own and caught hold of his hand with his other hand. He gathered all his force and kicked Flavius extremely hard on his chest.

The warrior fell like a chopped tree. Distantly, he heard his mother rushing towards him, crying, followed by the villagers.

The mask was removed from his face. Before he could collect his senses, Satrugna put his leg on his chest and dug his sword in the wound on Flavius' shoulder.

'My friend, it's our pride that helps us to grow, and as a warrior, I want to leave this earth, not as the vanquished but the vanquisher...' Flavius's words echoed in the ears of Elvin, who was crying uncontrollably, seeing Flavius lying in a pool of blood.

'Forgive me. I cannot separate your head from your body because you spared my life a few moments ago,' Satrugna whispered, looking at him.

A storm began to approach. The heavy wind filled the air with sand.

The old lady knelt beside her son's body.

'Maa, I'm defeated. This time, I failed to bring glory home. I'm sorry Maa...'

'No, son....' the old lady said, holding his hands with a broken heart. She couldn't seem to summon any more words.

'Maa, I promise you that I'll be your child when I again take birth on this earth again. I will fulfill all your wishes but for now, you have to forgive me for this death,' said Flavius.

The old lady was wiping her tears. Alishan arrived with the baby. Her eyes were big and moist. She moved to the mother's side, and unable to control herself, she stumbled on the ground.

'My love,' Flavius said in a faltering voice.

'No! You can't do this to me. You promised me that you wouldn't leave...'Alishan cried.

'Love...I beg you to forgive me for breaking my promise.'

'I can't live without you.... I shall die with you,' said Alishan, with love and tears in her eyes.

'No love, you must live for our love... our child. You have to keep your word.'

Both ladies were crying and shivering over the fate served to their family.

'Now promise me you will take our baby to a safe place. You'll have to leave this place, or else they will kill the symbol of our love,' he continued in a fading voice. 'This was a game... and I was trapped.' The shaking of his voice increased. 'The planners are Chief and Chandaliyan... They will kill him... Go! Leave this place.'

Both ladies raised their eyes. All was silent, and the lifeless body was lying still. Tears rolled from their eyes. The arena was celebrating the glory of the black-masked warrior, but the well-wishers of Flavius were silent. Then a loud cry echoed in the arena.

Following it, laughter echoed. 'I won, you're mine, come closer to me!' Saying this, the winning opponent held the crying Alishan's arms and lifted her up. ButAlishan couldn't feel it as her eyes were fixed on the body. The black-masked man tried to pull her *saree* and exploit her body, but because of the baby, the *saree* stayed in place. Feeling the obstruction of the baby, the masked man tried to pull her baby from her arms.

The baby started crying from the pain. Suddenly, Alishan's eyes grew bigger. She was furious and she turned around, pulling the sword from her husband's dead body. She slashed the masked man's arm. The hand fell to the ground, and the man howled in pain.

'How dare you touch me and my baby?' Her eyes were burning with fire. She adjusted her *saree*. 'Do you think every woman is weak?'

Satrugna gave instructions to his men to surround Alishan and get control over her, but she attacked one of them, and he was dead in one stroke. All the others stepped back. She turned around to take a last look at her husband's body, and throwing the sword away, she ran into the forest.

Chandaliyan's voice echoed in the arena. 'You cowardly villagers, what are you waiting for! Kill that baby, don't show mercy to that evil soul, or you will be responsible for your own destruction. He is a curse that will destroy the village. Find them and kill them both.'

Some villagers followed Alishan, carrying sticks in their hands. Other men followed carrying swords and axes on the Chief's instructions. They were searching in every possible direction, looking for a lone lady with an infant in her arms.

In the forest, one man asked Alishan, 'Please hand the child over to us. We've no intention to harm you. But we must kill the baby. It's a curse. It will ruin all of us.'

'No! I will not leave my child!'

'Give me the baby, Alishan. It's Elvin. I respect the mother in you, but it's a curse. Please try to understand. We have lost the great warrior because of this.'

Elvin caught hold of her from the back. He held the baby's cloth, but his hands slipped off, and he fell down on the ground and was unable to get up.

The lady shouted, 'Please leave him. He is innocent!'

Hurriedly, taking advantage of the dark, the woman hid behind a bush.

Suddenly a loud growl echoed in her ears. She held her baby tightly and opened her eyes to examine the shadow. It was a deadly dream, perhaps!

She saw a tiger moving towards her. She was shivering with fear. The cat went near the stone a few feet from the child and the lady. It caught a glimpse of the humans and started walking towards them.

7. THE DARK PROMISE

Dawn, the hour of silence. The rays filtering down through the dense forest ripped apart the darkness. Alishan's soul was burdened with a lot of darkness, annoyance and sorrow. The previous night's events still horrified her, and she was trying to revive from the horrible things she had dreamt about.

'This is my present situation…' said the dark figure, while stepping onto the place where the rays were falling.

'Please spare him…' holding her baby tightly, she was helplessly murmuring.

As the dark figure stood silhouetted against the light, Alishan's eyes moved from the lower extremity to the top. A man, barefoot and wearing a white loincloth, *kamandalu* in his left hand, coloured beads of various types in the other, a long white beard, some wrinkles on his face, long white hair, and a saffron cloth on shoulders, that was all she could see.

'Don't panic! You and your baby are secure. I'm not one of them,' the old saint said. 'The fear is past now, and you were reborn along with this small life. It was a dream.'

'Dream!'

'Yes… Sorrow is an endless journey that will remind you of your past. But at the same time, it will make you strong enough to stand alone. The journey will continue as long as you want to walk in the dreams of your past.'

'How can you interpret this so confidently, and say that I was dreaming?' Alishan asked.

'Life is hard to interpret. Wherever it takes us and no matter how dark and strenuous the time may be, whenever we close our eyes, we can dream and see flashbacks from our life.'

'I don't believe it. Who are you?'

'A common man, faithful to his notions, who loves nature… The beauty of the greenwood entices me. People say it's a jungle, but nature has convinced me to stay here, far from the village.'

The tiger stood up and went near the saint's feet and lowering its head, sat.

Alishan moved back on seeing the tiger's movement. The tiger roared.

'Stay back; he's the tiger that saved your life. He fought for you, unlike the others. He lives with me.' The old saint walked ahead and made himself comfortable on the big stone, followed by the tiger.

'Has he never hurt you?' Alishan asked.

'The animals are not meant for anyone. They breathe for themselves and are self-satisfied. They don't hurt anyone without reason. In these years, I have realised that if you want to awaken your soul, you have to love an animal, even if it is a wild one.'

'Your words are confusing, but I sense there is a story behind them…'

Swami Brahmanand coughed a bit, clearing his throat. He smiled and continued.

'It has been nearly eight years since I came to this greenwood for mental peace. I heard in another village that a man-eater walked these woods. It had killed many from the neighbouring villages. No one ever dared to come here alone. They came in groups with weapons. One day they took a decision, and they crossed the line of cruelty. They hired professional hunters to kill the beast. I endeavoured to manage the situation, but no one was in a state of mind to listen to me. So I decided to move to the forest before any mishap could take place. I continued my journey for years… but never found any tiger hunting humans. Only when a tiger grows old, then in order to fetch its prey, it hunts people.

'One night as I was strolling, I heard a deafening growl. I moved to the side from whence the sound was coming. As I headed to the place, I saw hunters holding lamps in their hands, also making their way to the source of the growl. I ran. As I approached, I saw a big tiger growling and crying, with six arrows pierced into his body. He was unable to move. Perhaps the hunters had left by that time. Again I heard the growl of a little one, somewhere nearby. My eyes searched and finally I found a cage, with a villager guarding it. I moved closer. There was a cub inside, trying to break free. I opened the cage, and it rushed out, seeking to find its mother.'

Swami Brahmanand rubbed his palm on the tiger's head.

'Just then I sensed the presence of the hunters. They approached me and were ready to kill the cub. In a commanding voice, I said, "Don't even think about it or else the consequences will be severe." "For your sake don't get angry, old man, we will not kill it. But we will take it with us. We'll sell it to the circus group in the city. We'll have some earnings. Some additional revenue, I mean. Don't you bother," they chuckled.

'I warn you…. Leave the cub or else I will turn you into ashes,' I said. I raised my water *kamandalu* and took some water in my other hand. They looked me in the eye. They left the cub and stepped back. As the hunters moved away, I took the cub in my hands and made way for it to reach its mother. As soon as the cub went closer, the mother regained some strength, and lifted her body and gave easy access for the cub to feed. While she was feeding her baby, she tried to lick it but was unable to do so because of the arrows and the pain. I took out all the arrows, one by one, and put some medicinal leaves on the wounds. This soothed her. By now she had understood that I was helping her. She didn't harm me. For a few days she lived, but due to her massive loss of blood, I couldn't save her. It took days for the cub to accept his mother's demise.

'The day was gleaming with warm sunshine when I opened my eyes. I saw the cub lying near my feet. From then on, it has been following me wherever I go. The animal showed gratitude for the help I had offered. Staying with me, it developed a sense of humanity, and now whenever it discerns any adversity, it comes forward to help others.'

'It seems this place is unsafe for my baby.' Saying this, Alishan held her baby and prepared to leave.

'Lady, I assure you that these woods are safer than the village you left behind. You stay here. Your safety is my duty, I promise, and besides this, there is a particular reason as well.' Saying this, Swami got up.

'A particular reason…?' Bewildered, Alishan raised her eyebrows.

Swami Brahmanand put his hands on the baby's head and closed his eyes 'The birth of this child was for a specific reason and he has to be protected unconditionally. He is destined to be a great warrior. Greater than his father. He will tear apart the evils of society. I need one promise from you.'

'What promise?'

'Promise me, until he is 22 years old, you will never let sun rays touch his skin. Also, don't ever cover his body.'

'But these conditions are impossible to fulfill, and it's still alright until he is independent. But once he is independent, how can I stop him?'

'Don't worry about that. I will be there with him, and I will train him to fulfil his destiny. But let me warn you too. You will also have to sacrifice a lot.'

The lady was confused about whether to rely on the sage or or not, so she remained silent. Swami continued:

'Have faith in me. I will never harm you.'

'Master, I promise I will never doubt your thoughts or question you.'

'Another thing: in my absence this tiger will guard both of you. I will visit you every day to see to your daily needs.' Saying this, the old man walked away with the tiger following him.

One evening, when Swamiji had yet to come, Alishan had no choice but to leave her sleeping baby on the straw in order to answer nature's call. The tiger was yawning at the entrance to the cave. While going out, the lady got confused about whether to leave her son alone or not, but the companionship shown by the tiger made her put all her doubts to rest. When Alishan returned, she heard a loud cry from the baby. She ran towards him, panicking.

The tiger was moving to and fro with the baby, growling and competing with the baby's loud cry. Alishan stumbled in shock and yelled, 'My baby, it will kill my baby… I knew it! I shouldn't have relied on a wild animal!'

Just then Swami entered. 'What happened lady, why are you yelling?'

She rushed towards Swami, held his hands and shouted, 'The animal will kill my baby. Please save him.'

'Have patience lady,' he said. The tiger was growling and playing with the baby.

'Your child is fine. The animal is growling out of affection, not anger. I understand it takes time to accept this reality. See, your baby is smiling now.'

Alishan raised her head and rushed to her child. She picked him up and kissed him all over. Seeing the truth of the situation, she felt guilty. She went to Swamiji and touched his feet and implored him to pardon her. Swami was disappointed by her accusation, and remained still. Alishan felt this and moved towards the tiger. She lowered her baby and placed him in front of the cat. The tiger lowered his head and licked the baby like his own cub.

'Never doubt our faith. Each and every moment is guided by the Almighty. This animal is here for the baby's protection, and it is doing its duty.'

A faint red colour was visible on the horizon and birds had begun screeching.

'It's twilight now; darkness is so abundant, am I right?' In a confident tone, Swami spoke: 'Darkness is all over, and entices you to give up. It's up to you whether you choose to believe in the Omnipotent, clutching to the ray of hope, or not.'

8. ACCEPTED AS DISCIPLE

Alishan lay beside her baby as the memories of yesteryear occupied her dreams. The voice of Flavius was still strong and clear in the corner of her heart and every night she would think of her husband and kiss the forehead of her child before going to sleep.

'Twilight, again… a new beginning…, the sun is yet to rise… Come with me Alishan, let me help you witness a miracle of sun and moon sharing the same sky. It's the time when the moon remains in the sky waiting for the sun to rise and bid goodbye till the next twilight… When we bid goodbye, it doesn't mean that we are parting from each other. Instead it means our paths will definitely cross, someday, somewhere,' Flavius whispered into her ears, showing her the red sky with the moon on one side, and the sun rising on the other.

She stared at the sun. The warmth of the rising sun left a smile on her lips. As the sight became blurred, she closed her eyes and rested her head on Flavius's shoulder. Warm tears rolled down her cheeks despite the smile on her lips.

'This very moment speaks the truth. Why do we never know what we have till it is gone? Absence makes us understand how special the moments spent together were. It's the law of nature. Now look me in the eye. It's time to bid farewell.' Alishan opened her eyes to find her body covered in sweat.

'Open your eyes Alishan. It's time to start the new phase of life.' Swami's voice roused her further.

It was still dark outside. Alishan rubbed her eyes, and saw there was a figure approaching the cave. She stood up adjusting her *saree*.

Alishan followed Swami Brahmanand towards the east. Swamiji stopped at a spot. It seemed to be a dried pond, surrounded by bushes and trees.

'Step in with folded hands, keeping the boy on your shoulder, and purify your body by taking a bath.'

Alishan looked confused while stepping into the pond. Seeing this, Swamiji smiled and said:

'Don't fear; do as per my instructions… and repeat after me:

Om apavitrahpavitrova

Sarvavastamgatoapiva

Yabsmaretpundarikaksam

Sabahyaabhyantaramsudhi

Sri Vishnu sri Vishnu sri Vishnu

As the lady finished chanting, she felt a cold tickling sensation under her feet. She opened her eyes to see what had happened. Water was rising from inside the earth. She was astonished seeing the dried pond getting filled with clear water. She looked to Swamiji for an explanation.

He asked her to take a bath in the holy pond named 'Madhu-Pushkarini' and then left after giving her some instructions.

The rising water soaked her, and felt as though the divinities were bathing her themselves. Alishan was shivering with cold as she stepped out of the pond. With every step, she looked back to find the water level decreasing drastically. As she moved forward, she saw water escaping back into the earth from the very pores it had seeped out of.

Henceforth each day, the lady would enter the pond, her child on her shoulder, hands folded and eyes closed, in the manner told to her by Swami. She and her baby would take a bath and go back.

'Purifying your soul should be the beginning to explore the destination, so after a bath, we should ask destiny to cleanse our soul, and erase evil from our minds.' Swami's instructions formed the bedrock of her life.

All her necessities like food, clothing and shelter were being taken care of by Swamiji. She had blind faith which made her never question him. She never felt an urge to ask and most of the time she received answers without asking. And to some questions, all she got was an expression on Swami's face saying without words 'Believe in the Almighty, have patience.'

Four years passed.

It was a Guru-Poornima day, and the sun was yet to rise. Alishan remembered what Swami had told her: this day, he would accept her son as his disciple. With love, she moved her fingers over his son's face and kissed his forehead. Then she heard someone chanting mantras:

'KarpuraGauramKarunavataram

Samsara SaramBhujagendraHaaram

SadaaVasantamHrdayaAravinde

BhavamBhavaaniiSahitamNamaami

BhavamBhavaaniiSahitamNamaami'

She was surprised by the voice at this time of day.

She tried following the direction of the sound. And finally, she saw an unbelievable sight. Behind the cave, there was a Natraj idol about fifteen feet high, and a man was dancing and doing Shiva Tandav before it. He was dancing, crying, and smiling at the same time. He was dancing to impress his Lord, crying to convey his message to his master, telling Him that people were suffering, and smiling in respect to his destiny, to accept his fate.

From the entrance of the cave, she noticed that he was wet from the trickling water inside the cave without any origin. It was quite strange for the lady, to see him like this. After he had taken bath, with folded hands, he closed his eyes and chanted some mantras. Then he looked up and whispered something, watching the tree above him. And, suddenly the branch of the tree with red flowers bent down, showing respect to his words. The man plucked some flowers and smiled at the branch, acknowledging it and thanking it. The branch quietly moved back to its original place. The man offered the flowers at the feet of the deity. Then he knelt down before his god.

Seeing all this, Alishan was astonished.

'He is not an ordinary man, as I assumed at first. If what I have seen just now is true…' whispered Alishan to herself. She moved back, thinking it would be awkward if the Swami were to see her watching him. She came back to her son. She closed her eyes for a while, thinking about the scenes that she just seen, and wondered about Swami's true nature.

When she heard the tiger growling, she lost her concentration. She picked up her son, being a bit more cautious. Just then her son opened his eyes and smiled.

'It's time, Ma. Shall we purify our bodies?' he asked.

'Yes… a new life is going to start. You are going to learn about the essence of life. I was waiting for this day to come, my son.' Alishan kissed his forehead, and both of them went to take a bath in the holy pond.

After taking a bath, they followed the path to Swamiji, expecting more surprises.

'It's time Alishan. Destiny has waited for four years. It's time for the boy to follow his remarkable path. Come with me.'

Swamiji moved outside to the back of cave, pushing the bushes aside. This was where she had seen him praying.

'Move fast, the sun has risen!' Swamiji said.

He made himself comfortable in front of the idol and asked them to take their places next to him. Alishan settled down with her son in her lap.

'Today is that special day, Guru Purnima. Today I declare your child to be my disciple.' Swamiji closed his eyes and chanted some mantras, folding his hands.

'Your child will be known to the world as Aryan.' Tying a sacred thread around his wrist, Swamiji spoke. Alishan smiled and murmured 'Aryan...my baby,' and kissed her son's cheeks. Aryan was looking at the Natraj idol. Swamiji ordered him to stand up.

The child was not acquainted with his new name, so he seemed confused. Alishan stood up holding her child's hand and moved closer to Swamiji.

'Aryan, join your hands together and repeat what I say.'

Alishan knelt and joined the hands of Aryan at the height of his chest.

'*Aum...*' Closing his eyes, Swamiji began.

Alishan asked Aryan to close his eyes and repeat the word. Aryan, Alishan and Swamiji recited once again. The '*Aum*' echoed in the forest.

'Now open your eyes, and get down on your knees with folded hands. Alishan, bow your head and ask the Almighty to purify your mind, as well as that of your son.'

Alishan bowed her head in front of the idol, prayed with eyes closed and her hands folded. The baby followed her example.

'Lady, turn this side. Aryan, come closer.'

Alishan instructed the boy to obey, and he knelt in front of Swamiji, mischievous expressions mixed with confusion on his face. He was restless, but his mother instructed him to stay still.

Aum...Gurur brahma

Gurur Vishnu

Gurur deva maheswaram

Gururshakshatparam brahma

Tasmaiyeeshreeguravenamah…

Alishan and Aryan chanted the mantra, and Aryan's immature pronunciation displayed the innocence in his heart. Alishan opened her eyes and bent her head, and so did Aryan. Swamiji showered flowers and white rice mixed with turmeric on them and then asked them to get up.

Swamiji took some vermillion on his thumb and index finger and put it on Aryan and Alishan's foreheads. Then he took out a small knife from his belt. Alishan looked at it in confusion. Swamiji held Aryan's hand and pulled him close. He then asked him to sit in his lap for further proceedings. With his knife, he shaved Aryan's head, making him completely bald.

The child had started crying and tried to move out of the grip of Swamiji's hand, but was unable to. Swamiji cleared his head, removing even the smallest of hairs, and then left him. Aryan rushed towards his mother and hugged her tightly with his small hands. Swamiji lifted his *kamandalu*and took some water in his hand and sprinkled it on himself and then some on the child and the mother. As water fell over the child, he stopped crying and looked up in curiosity. While sprinkling water, Swamiji murmured some mantras, his eyes closed.

After the completion of the formalities, Swamiji accepted him as his disciple.

Alishan bowed, and so did Aryan. Swamiji stood up and blessed both of them: 'May the Lord protect you from all the evil powers. Now both of you go quickly into the cave. The sun has begun to rise. Don't let the light touch the boy.'

9. DARKNESS IS YOUR FATE!

Swamiji moved away from the cave. The sunrays pierced the forest and the glow at the entrance of the cave attracted the child. He started trotting towards it but Alishan caught hold of him and lifted him up. 'Darkness is your fate my son,' she said and stepped back, looking with terror at the brightening entrance.

Aryan grew acquainted with his new name and even got used to the dark. After all, Nature has bestowed upon us a very powerful capacity for adaptation. It became quite easy for him to move in the dark. Alishan changed her own routine to suit Aryan's, going to sleep at dawn and getting up at dusk. Slowly, their lives fell into a pattern.

Swamiji came every evening, with the approaching darkness. He taught Aryan first how to make the unstable mind stable. He taught him that '*Aum*' is the word in which the origin of the world is defined. He told him to close his eyes and find a point in the darkness. Focusing on it, he was to breathe regularly, drawing the sound of 'Aum' from his navel. This regular practice brought stability to Aryan, which was reflected in his work. He remained calm. Swamiji felt the boy was getting ready for more teachings as an obedient disciple.

AumBhurvuvahswah

Tat saviturvarenyam

Bhargodevasyadhimayi

Dhiyoya nah prachodayat

Closing his eyes, Swamiji chanted the mantra. When he opened his eyes and was about to elaborate on the meaning, he saw something different and unusual. Aryan didn't imitate the words. His eyes were stuck on the thick red cloth wrapped around Swamiji's waist.

'Aryan?' he asked.

Aryan looked at him with his innocent gaze dancing to and fro between the red cloth and Swamiji's face. Swamiji realized that the child was growing and so was his mind; he was curious about his waist cloth. He ordered Aryan to close eyes, fold his hands and recite the word '*Aum*'. As Aryan started his chanting, Swamiji stood up and left; from somewhere a little ahead from the entrance to the cave, he started shouting and so did the tiger, which had followed him.

'Why? My Lord… how can someone be considered a curse, that too an innocent child who hardly knows this world!'

Alishan tried to eavesdrop from inside the cave, but was unable to hear anything clearly except 'Why?' and 'My Lord'. The other words were lost.

Swamiji roared, 'I don't have the strength to face this reality, how can I tell them the truth of what destiny wants from them?' He knelt down. Suddenly, water droplets made their way through the dense forest, falling from the clouds. Swamiji got soaked to the bones and was shivering. The tiger was roaring now in an unusual fashion, and getting drenched along with him. After some time, Swamiji regained his strength and walked into the cave, followed by the tiger. He stopped at the entrance. 'Alishan....'

Alishan went to him and stood before him with folded hands. Aryan was chanting '*Aum*' from his navel. He was focused on his chanting in such a way that, for him, nothing was visible or audible except '*Aum*' and the white spot in the darkness.

'Now the time has come to sacrifice once more for your child. This sacrifice will be the toughest for you. You have to sacrifice your cloth from today on for fifteen years,' Swamiji said in an uncomfortable manner, turning his face aside.

Hearing this, Alishan stepped back, holding her torn *saree* tightly and looking confusedly, helplessly at him.

'From today on you must remain undressed in front of your child, and you will have to continue this for fifteen years. This may be awkward for you, but this is your fate,' Swamiji said boldly.

'Guruji... please have mercy on me... this is impossible. How can I stay bare in front of you and my child? Not for a single moment could I do this, and fifteen long years...! I'm a lady. I can never even think about it. I'm dedicated my love, my husband still, and except for him I could never show my body to another man. I would rather face death than do this. Please have mercy. I can't do this.' Alishan fell to her knees.

Swami Brahmanand stepped ahead, and stretched his hands towards Alishan. Alishan raised her eyes, when she saw him, she was frightened. She glanced at Aryan and then turned her face towards

Swamiji, holding her clothing tightly and looking helpless.

Swamiji put his hand over her head.

'You need to sacrifice your clothing in front your child, not me. The reason for this sacrifice is your child. He is going to be seven years old in a few days. His attraction towards clothing will rise day by day and to avoid this, we need to avoid clothes altogether.'

Alishan tried to come at terms with it, but she couldn't.

'I've a way out of this embarrassing situation. Not only you, even I will have to remain naked in front of Aryan. When the darkness appears you will have to leave before your son wakes up. I'll be there with him the whole time, and while entering the cave I will unclothe myself. After I have taken leave, just before twilight, you may enter the cave undressed. But before entering you must have taken a bath in Madhu – Puskarini.'

'But how can I live this way for fifteen long years? After some time, he will grow into manhood, and he will remain no longer a child. It will be very embarrassing,' Alishan said in a worried voice.

'Your child is far away from emotion and attractions. Nothing is hidden from a creator. A child is born nude. There is no relation as pure as that between a mother and child. If this practice is observed from childhood then even after gaining maturity, Aryan will not have the feelings you predict. But one thing is to be strictly taken care of: he must never come in contact with the exterior world, pleasure or sunlight. His world must consist of you, his guru and the tiger. You must continue the routine you have set yourself.'

Alishan whispered, 'How is this possible? How can a grown up remain completely naked in front of his mother!'

She looked at Aryan, who was still chanting.

'What has destiny decided for us?'

For the time being, she thought of covering herself with leaves but then some random thoughts from yesteryears changed her mind. She recalled the story of Duryodhan and his mother.

'What have you done Duryodhan? I asked you to come to me completely bare. Why have you covered yourself with a banana leaf? The part you have covered up will be your weakness; the parts of your body which are bare will be of bajra. No weapon will harm the parts that I have seen, but the covered part will make you vulnerable,' said Gandhari.

'But I am a grown man, how could I come in front of you completely bare?'

'Son, a child is born naked and nothing is hidden from a mother. Now nothing can be done. Your groin will remain weak when the whole body has turned to *bajra*. The boon I got for worshiping Lord Shiva with my blindfolded eyes could only be used once.'

These stories echoed in Alishan's ears. She went out of the cave and took off her clothing, and hid it behind a bush. When she came back inside the cave, she went to her son and put her hands on his shoulders.

'Aryan, son, it's time to sleep.'

Aryan opened his eyes and looked at his mother. He knew there was something different about her, but he was not sure what it was. Putting it out of his mind, he went to sleep.

At the approach of darkness, when he opened his eyes, he didn't find his mother. Instead, he found Swamiji waiting for him.

'Aryan, get up.' Even Swamiji looked different. The red waistcloth was not there anymore. There were only beads hanging around his neck and a bracelet tied around his wrist. But Aryan was unsure of what to say, so he remained silent.

Swamiji looked up, closed his eyes and thanked his Lord for having allowed him to escape the awkward questions he had anticipated. They settled in one place and started their chanting: '*Aum*'.

10. Fate decides to unite souls!

It was sometime between midnight and dawn. Alishan, covering her face with the *pallu* of her *saree*, was roaming near the cave. She was collecting fruits and flowers for the next morning. Suddenly, she heard a sound and curious, started walking towards it. It was dark, and she was unable to see clearly. The only thing visible was a big lamp hanging at a distance, hoisted at the top of a bamboo hut.

When she approached, she saw some idols made of clay. A white-haired old man was giving shape to a big idol. She stared at it and smiled. She recalled her first meeting with Flavius.

Alishan was only sixteen. Her laborious routine had given her strength and a shape which could make the most beautiful of princesses jealous. Her complexion was tanned from working in the sunlight on clay and sculptures. Her hands were caked with mud, and she was trying to shape an idol of Krishna. Her shoulders were bare. All she was wearing was a rough, dark *saree*, covering the essential parts of her body.

Suddenly, she noticed someone staring at her. She felt awkward but avoided looking at first. She continued doing her job, but the man didn't move. She collected herself and questioned him.

'Who are you? What makes you stay here?'

'Your art, the way you sculpt the idol is impressive. Would you mind making one of me? I would pay you a fair price.' The fine built, broad shouldered man had mischief and tenderness in his eyes.

'No one can pay an artist's wage. We only ask for a small fare in return, so that we can make a living.'

'You can ask me for anything in return. I hope I won't disappoint you.'

'My family includes just my father and me. We are clay artists. But I can't imagine putting your image in a work of art because I am a girl.'

'How does that make sense?'

'I can't think of a man and then create an idol of him. I have to keep my eyes on you. If I do so, I will have to end up marrying you, as in my culture, thinking of or imagining a man is only permissible if the girl is getting married to him. Even if I don't have any ill-intentions, I am compelled to disappoint you.'

'But I won't leave this place until you agree to my request.'

'Don't force me to call my father. He is not only a clay artist but a terrific archer too. Now you choose, whether you want to save your own life, or take a risk by standing here.'

'I am here for a valid reason. Being a warrior, I am not afraid of death. Rather, I choose this path, as it is, to me, the ultimate truth. I believe that if you can't achieve your dream, it's better to close your eyes. So long as I live, I will dare to dream!'

'Little girl, what are you doing there?' Alishan's father came out of the hut.

Alishan ran towards her father and told him of the situation. Syombhu Murthy approached Flavius.

'Who are you?' he asked.

'I am Flavius, a warrior of the city of Satwaparvat.'

'You are a warrior, and a warrior is a respectable figure. Don't you think your wandering and intruding onto someone's property might dampen your fame?'

'I fight for myself, not for fame. And admiring something isn't a mistake in any way. A great person can only admire something great.'

'I have seen more of this world than you. These old eyes have seen the worst of things that came his way. You might try to hide your intention, but it can't escape my eyes. Admiring something is good, but achieving something you admire is up to destiny. You admire her work, do you admire her beauty?'

'I do...' Flavius replied.

'I knew it. I have been at your age; you can't cheat this old man. Achieving what you admire is a matter of your destiny! Here your fate is 'I'. You have to face the most difficult exam of your life; if you succeed at it, your dreams will be accepted by destiny. If not...'

'Accepted...' Flavius was all set to face the future. Alishan's eyebrows rose. She grew worried thinking of the consequences!

'What made you stay here?' the old voice disturbed Alishan's thoughts, and she came back to reality. She was standing near a bamboo hut, in front of an old man.

'Your art is impressive.'

'Do you live nearby?' asked the old man. The old man thought she looked familiar.

'Don't believe the people nearby. Avoid exposing your identity. That will be right for you and your baby.' Before Alishan could reply to the old man, she recalled Swamiji's advice and stopped. At once, she ran away.

'Now what should I do? Meeting him like this, was it destined?' Alishan asked herself. She turned back. The old man was walking towards the bamboo hut. He was unable to walk properly. His weakness convinced Alishan break her promise to Swamiji. She moved back towards the man, and held his shoulder to help him sit.

'Do you recognise me…?' Alishan asked, showing her face and raising her eyebrows.

At the breaking of dawn, Swamiji asked Aryan to follow him. That day they went near Madhu –Puskarini using a different route.

Swamiji asked Aryan to take the path to where his mother would be waiting for him, and Aryan did as directed. He rushed ahead, and Swamiji put on the clothes he had hidden behind a stone.

 On the way, he met Alishan and stopped.

'I am afraid. I do not know if I have done the right thing,' Alishan said, shivering.

'You have broken your promise,' Swami said.

'I tried not to, but…'

'It happens when it's destined to happen! We can't control our emotions when we see our near and dear ones.'

'He is suffering from memory loss.' cried Alishan, and told him the story.

'You are a lady residing in this forest, that's all I can guess,' answered the old man.

Alishan took his hand and started pressing it as she had used to do years earlier.

'I am feeling something, but I don't know what it is! Years back…' the old man stopped speaking and started crying. 'Forgive me, lady, I can't…'

Alishan hugged him tightly and whispered in his ears, 'Father…'

The old man coughed and started staring at her. Pointing his index finger, he was trying to say, 'You are lying, they killed her.'

He started crying, and Alishan pressed his head with affection and tried to tell him her story, but it seemed that the old man was not ready to listen. He turned away, showing his back to Alishan.

'This is Alishan, your daughter. She is alive, believe me, Father.'

'For many years, I have not seen my daughter. How can I trust you?'

'Look in my eyes, father. This is the same Alishan who used to make clay idols with you, and you used to say no one can take away your art. You are the sole owner of it. Everything is temporary, but your art, learning, impression is what remains; people talk about it even after your death!'

The old man turned back, stared at her and raised his shivering hands to touch her face. He was trying to find his daughter in her, and Alishan was trying to show her affection for her father. She helped him to recall it all, and the old man started to smile and begin to get up.

'My daughter...' he hugged her like a child.

-=-=-=-=-=-

'I tried and succeeded, but he forgot me after a while again. I am sure that he is suffering from memory loss.'

Alishan looked into the eyes of Swami. He was standing still.

'I am sorry to have done this without your permission...'

'A girl needs no permission to meet his father! Though you have broken your promise, I understand your concern for your father. Whatever happens happens for a reason. Emotions have no boundaries, and they can't be controlled. Leave it, now it's time for you to return to your child. He is alone and must be looking for you. You should go now,' Swami commanded, and Alishan left.

11. Feminine strikes the Empire

Kumbhgarh, the capital of Chief Mathews.

He had shifted to this new capital six years earlier after marrying Seliana, daughter of the former king Mani Kumbh. The Kumbh Empire was at its height, and with time the number of their slaves had grown in lakhs. Lack of literacy, poverty, shelter made them sick and they agreed to sell themselves and their child to the Chief. They served as slaves, and in some places they were used as entertainers. In others, they fought for the growth of the Empire, like Flavius had!

The audience was happy and the entire arena was echoing with sounds of pleasures and cries of torment. It was a day of celebration. All the slaves were celebrating their day as Chief Mathews had been able to conquer one more city, named Suvarna. It was the day to celebrate glory; blood had turned the battleground red, and animals were sliced into pieces to munch on. Burning wood served the purpose of frying the flesh, women slaves were dancing and entertaining the huge crowd in the arena. Chandaliyan was consuming wine while enjoying it all. Mathews declared, standing on the high ground, 'It's your day, all these women are yours, irrespective of whether they are wife, daughter or sister of anyone else. Your hunger for pleasure is all that they are here to serve! Likewise, any woman has the freedom to choose the man she wants to bed. The choice is all yours: choice of food, choice to fulfil your bodily needs and choice to enjoy the day!'

The crowd roared and threw wine on each other, some out of happiness and some out of anger. A few men started pulling the other men's ladies and started fighting. Men approached women, tore their clothes off and started having sex with them there itself. Left without a choice, the ladies became submissive to the greedy men.

'Fuck! Fuck hard! Fuck or else get fucked up!' Chandaliyan roared, encouraging the crowd.

Those with moral and societal values pulled their swords out in protest. Blood was flowing like water, men and women were lying bare and playing with blood and skins. Cannibalism overtook them completely and men lost their humanity to it.

This culture continued to serve Chief Mathews. The game was extended from Satwaparwat to Kumbhgarh and the more than hundreds of cities the Chief had conquered. A selfish man by nature, greedy to expand his Empire, he had never hesitated to play with blood. His paramour Marina Soni used to support him in these acts. He would meet her secretly without Seliana's knowledge.

'Even I want to make children and live the life of a normal village man, but it's impossible now...' shouted the slave AhimSoni, husband of Marina Soni.

'I dreamt of much more than you gave me,' Marina wept, sitting on her wooden bed.

'Girls die to bed the Chief. Your beauty has served us for the last five years, so I am obliged to you. But desire is something that never ends. It's like a poison. When it reaches extremes, either you die or you end up getting addicted. He is addicted to you, and in return we can award him death.' Standing near her, Ahim whispered in her ears.

'We have been serving him for years; for his entertainment, we have been parted from each other.'

'I promised you that we will be awarded freedom soon, but if you agree to do what I say. It all depends on you!'

At that moment, the Chief entered.

'It's time to bid your wife goodbye,' said the Chief. Ahim left the place without a word.

Though Marina was not happy, she had to wear a fake smile in front of the Chief, so she did.

'I can serve your desire, your hunger... Come to me, my love.'

She slipped out of her velvet gown and licked her lips provocatively. Mathews made himself comfortable on her bed. She undressed him and offered him wine. He consumed it and then started taking his pleasure with her.

'You have given me such amazing nights...'

'Your wife will be expecting you. Being a woman, I feel this is wrong.'

'She is different from you. She is happy with her child, her family, name and fame. I don't interfere with her and she returns the favour by not interfering with me! But all you need is a safe place to live, and see… you are in my arms, the safest place of all.'

'You promised to award me a home in Suvarna City, my Lord,' said Marina.

'Oh… your greed is growing day by day. I can see that. What will you do there? Are you looking for freedom? I can't free you just like that! You have to fulfil my bodily desires till the time I am bored of you.'

Ahim was standing behind the transparent screen and watching his wife, feeling undone.

After a long time, Mathews came out of the room. He saw Ahim waiting outside. His eyes were blood red with anger while the Chief's eyes were glowing with satisfaction.

'I hope she enjoyed herself as much as I did,' the Chief said, and smiled with pride.

Ahim came running inside, held his wife and cried.

Seliana was kept in the dark about all of this: the slavery, her husband's depravities. She was quite clear in her thoughts. Her way of thinking as a King's daughter and Chief's wife was entirely different and she believed in humanity and justice. Her voice was quite sharp and whatever she said, she meant it word for word. She always did her best to fulfill her promises.

She lived a life of habits; after taking a bath, dressing up in a well draped orange *saree*, she would walk towards the Sati Temple with a well decorated *pooja thali* and a bowl of milk. On the way to the temple, she would meet a donkey standing on the road. She used to feed that donkey and then continue to the temple. Commoners who met her on the way showed her love and respect by bending down. Seliana in return smiled at everyone. After offering prayers in the temple she would go to an anthill, home to two big cobras. Seliana would put the milk bowl down near the anthill and close her eyes, fold her hands, and moments later both the cobras would come out of the anthill and sip all the milk. They would leave their venom behind. She carried this to her palace.

On one particular day, some tribal men and women had gathered outside the palace, anger in their eyes. All of them were grunting, brandishing axes and sticks. The guards outside requested them to stop sloganeering and not to enter the palace. A lady inside the palace was sitting on a golden-plated lavish bed. She seemed to be very restless as she was constantly twisting her hands.

Just then a maid rushed into the room.

'Madam! The tribals, they are unstoppable, they're burning with anger...'

The restless lady lifted herself up and rushed towards an almirah. She picked up a blue bottle and a glass from inside. She poured some liquid into the glass.

'Madam... venom!' the maid squealed.

'Venom represents the evil sources all around. Accepting it with a pure soul and good intentions, it will provide you strength to stand against evil.' Seliana spoke in a sharp and confident voice. Her appearance and sharpness was quite unique and appealing at that moment. Her blue eyes were glaring now and her tongue was almost blue. Her hair was untied and she was shivering in anger. She lifted the glass to her lips and closed her eyes. She turned her face towards the maid. The maid was terrified and sweating. As the venom completely drained into Seliana's throat, she lowered the glass and opened her eyes. Now she appeared calm and composed. Her eyes glowed with self-confidence. She moved out of the room quickly, followed by the maid. As she was moving in the corridor, she met Mathews.

'Where are you going, Chief?' asked Seliana boldly.

Slowing down, looking towards the lady, he replied, 'It's none of your business.' He was about to move ahead when he stopped to hear her say, 'It is my business; I've the same rights as you.'

Mathews' temper was raised but as the maid and his kinsmen were present, he didn't utter a word. He glanced at them and finally looked towards Seliana and brushed his finger tips on the edges of his moustache. Seliana clapped two times. Instantly, the two kinsmen and the maid bowed their heads and stepped back.

'Your expressions say something, Chief.'

'Nothing. It is none of your business.'

'I know the solution; I am just trying to figure out the cause. Will you help me understand the cause?'

'You need not worry as I've figured out what has to be done.'

'Chandaliyan is not the solution; rather he is the reason behind your challenges.' Seliana raised her eyes and tried convincing him. 'Wait, don't do this. Aren't we courageous enough to face these tribes and their issues! Then why involve him?'

'I will ask Chandaliyan to burn this tribal group to ashes and with the ashes the issue shall fly away in the air.'

'What is the issue?'

'They are demanding that I give them farming land.'

'Oh... so your land is the issue. Let me handle this.'

Mathews chuckled. 'You will handle this; I don't want you to come in my way, please...'

'My father used to say we can't conquer the world with hatred and the sword, rather we can do so through love and affection.'

Seliana turned towards the entrance to the palace. 'Wait!' Mathews shouted, but she had already gone ahead.

12. Transparency defines Intellectuality

Seliana came out of the palace, and as soon as the tribals saw her approaching, they lowered their heads in respect and fell silent. Amongst the men, she saw the donkey that she used to feed every morning, who was braying aloud.

Seliana ordered the guards to allow the group to come up the stairs.

A few men and women from the group came running and fell at her feet. Seliana asked them to rise and asked them to state their problems. The very same moment, Mathews reached and stood by the door, and watched the interaction.

'Madam… please have mercy on us,' one of the women cried with folded hands.

One of the men who seemed to be the head of the clan said, 'Madam, our clan has been farming the land for ages. We used to pay half of our earnings to the Chief, your father. Before his dismissal, he gave his word that he would legally transfer the land to us. After his death, we continued the deal with his son-in-law, the present Chief, as per your father's words. We have asked the new Chief many times for the legal transfer of the land, and every time he has delayed the same. Then he raised the tax to three fourth of the earnings. With the hope that after legal transfer we would not have to pay the farm revenue, we accepted his condition. But, now he is asking us to pay our entire earnings. Tell us what we should do.'

'You all have to agree to my deal or else leave my land. If you don't, then the consequences will be severe,' thundered the Chief.

'We will not leave. We will not leave our farming land, our working land!' all the men and women cried.

'Your land? You outcasts are not equal to my body's dirt. Your land! Damn, now that's too much.'

'Ma'am, please say something!'

'You must all leave the land,' Seliana said.

The Chief chuckled and started brushing his long moustache. Seliana looked behind and saw Mathews smiling as if he had achieved what he wanted.

'Madam! No madam, please don't say this. We have expectations of you.'

'I will stick to what I have said. You leave this land, and in return, I will give you ten acres of land on the river bank, and you need not pay anything for this. Move there and settle there in peace. I will see to it that no one disturbs you.'

The tribals cried out with joy. Many of them fell at her feet, while the Chief burnt in anger.

'Now all of you pack your belongings and get moving. I will get the legal procedures done and send my word with the declarations and guide you to the new place.'

The men and women thanked the lady for her kind act and moved back to their dwellings joyfully.

'What is this? How can you donate the land without my permission?' the Chief thundered.

She replied, 'This is what is called justice. I don't need your authorization to donate my land. Maybe now you will understand. Your farm earnings will be stopped. Is this not a massive loss?' And she walked back inside the palace.

The Chief was speechless with anger.

(Satwaparvat Jungle, mid-day)

The tiger came out of the cave with a roar.

Inside the cave, Aryan was sitting beside his mother. He asked, 'Maa, I want to ask you something. Recently I have noticed something unusual about you and Guruji'.

A bird came inside the cave and started singing. Aryan got distracted and began moving towards it. He had gone a few steps ahead when Alishan stopped him. 'Son, you have to promise me that you will never step out of this cave alone.'

'Maa, let's go out and catch it,' Aryan pulled Alishan by her hand, ignoring her words.

'It's time to sleep, dear. Have some fruits, and go to bed.'

But Aryan, being stubborn and childish, tried to move ahead. He was held back firmly by Alishan. She handed him a guava. Aryan ate it and lay down to sleep, but was once again caught by his mother. Alishan moved her hands on his head and kissed his forehead and asked him to sleep. This time, Aryan obeyed her and closed his eyes and lay still.

'Today, the question has struck his mind. For how long can it be avoided? Today, the bird saved me. What does fate hold for me? Why are we cursed to live like this? We are cursed to remain completely bare for fifteen years. Even Guruji will be suffering for fifteen years,' Alishan whispered to herself.

'Why has the fate decided our journey would turn out this way...' Helplessly, her eyes closed.

After a few moments, Aryan opened his eyes, looking out towards the world. The sun woke him up. He slowly moved his mother's hand away from his chest and joyously stepped towards the entrance. His eyes closed a bit because he had never seen such bright light.

His eyes were acquainted with darkness. He was unable to keep his eyes open; brightness was hurting him. He covered his eyes with his hands and came closer to the entrance. He was smiling and eager to explore the world beyond darkness. Suddenly, the tiger jumped from the top of the cave and turned back towards the entrance. Aryan stopped for a moment at the sudden blockage and then continued moving out. The tiger kept coming towards the cave. As Aryan was about to step outside the cave, the tiger roared. Aryan grew frightened and astonished at this strange behaviour of the cat, who had never dared to harm him. It had never roared in such a way. He grew so frightened that he slipped and fell yelling out, 'Maaaa!'

Astonished, Alishan got up from her sleep. 'Aryan!' she yelled. Quickly, she moved towards them, crawling back inside with the tiger growling furiously. As she approached and grasped the child, the tiger started to calm down.

'Maa, I was trying to jump. It roared loudly. I got frightened,' Aryan replied, stammering.

'Aryan, why were you near the entrance? You were supposed to sleep next to me.'

'I was going out. I'm frightened Maa,' Aryan continued.

'Son, don't fear, this tiger won't harm you. Once it saved both our lives, and now it prohibited you from going out, that's it. Aryan, I had asked you to promise me that you would never step out alone and particularly in the daytime.'

'Why Maa, why can't I go? At night everything seems black, but during the day, all things appear differently,' argued Aryan.

'Guruji has asked us to follow this rule; neither you nor I can step out. If you want to disobey Guruji, then go ahead.'

'But what is the reason behind it?'

'There is a reason behind everything, but sometimes asking the reason at a wrong time might create disbelief. He is your Guru, he won't disappoint you, and you should have patience.'

'I promise you, I will never step out of the cave at daytime without your permission.'

Both the mother and son moved to their rock bed and went to sleep. Aryan held his mother tightly, trying to forget the tiger's loud roar.

Days passed, and Aryan kept his promise. He never dared to step out, but his curiosity never faded. Swamiji marked this change. To divert his thoughts and teach him how to concentrate, he started giving him yoga lessons. Every day, Swamiji taught Aryan one 'asana' and its usefulness. Aryan was a fast learner and with the guidance of Swami

Brahmanand, he soon mastered all the forms of yoga.

'Yoga adds strength and beauty to our body, mind and soul. It can mould you to achieve the height that great heroes of our past reached. Every mantra has its virtues. Mantras are recited not only to perform prayers or rituals but to refine your speech and help in fighting diseases as well,' Swamiji said.

'How can they fight internal diseases?' Aryan asked with folded hands.

'Pronunciation of mantras in *shudh* Sanskrit creates a vibration in the body and brain, which guides the flow of energy in the body. You can take the example of a conch. When you blow air into it, a pleasant sound comes out, which is loved by the heavenly bodies. No prayer is complete without this sound. It even cures irritation in the throat, cold, cough, eyesight and heart problems. Every matter found in this world is useful in one or more ways. You should never underestimate others.'

Aryan nodded, paying respect to Swamiji's words.

13. Beyond the Darkness

With time Aryan had learned more than expected from Swami Brahmanand. He was now well versed in Sanskrit mantras. His mind, body and soul had adapted to these regular lessons. Swamiji was very satisfied so he decided to move a step ahead with his training.

'Now the time has come for you to know more about the exterior world, the world beyond this cave. I know you have always longed to explore it. Come, follow me.' Swamiji marched ahead, and Aryan followed him with folded hands. His face and eyes were glowing with excitement. For the very first time, he was going to explore an unknown world. So far, he had been out with Swamiji to Madhu–Puskarini, but beyond that he had never been allowed to venture.

That night there was a full moon. The world seemed to be sparking. Swamiji stepped out of the cave, and Aryan followed with raised eyes and a smiling face.

'Aryan, the night is yours. Go! Feel it, let them know you are here to love them, the night, the birds, the animals, the wind, the moon, tell everyone!' Swamiji announced energetically.

Aryan bowed and sought his blessings by touching Swamiji's feet. Then he walked with great excitement. A cool wind was blowing through the forest. With closed eyes, he felt the air and breathed long. That night, Swamiji left Aryan free in the new world that he had desired to feel, to know. Aryan tried to get closer to the world. The tiger followed his every step. Swami Brahmanand was happy to see his disciple so happy, enjoying the vast world in the moonlight.

Alishan was strolling in the forest and collecting some food when she heard a voice. She hid behind a big tree, its stem covered with creepers. She peeped out to see the source of the noise. She saw a boy roaming around in the moonlight, completely naked, followed by a tiger.

She was confused and afraid. 'How come Aryan is outside the cave? Where is Guruji? It's his time to be with him. Has something happened?'

She was about to go to him, but she stopped thinking, 'Right now I'm draped in a *saree*, what if Aryan sees this? Then unnecessary questions will disturb his mind.'

Just then, she heard Swamiji's voice calling out for Aryan some distance away. As they heard Swamiji's voice, the tiger growled, and both of them stopped, realising it was a call to return. Both of them moved towards the voice and Alishan, maintaining distance followed them.

On the way to the cave's entrance, Swamiji held a stick and hit it against Aryan's palm. 'What do you feel Aryan?' Swamiji asked.

'It hurts,' replied Aryan.

'This pain you felt is new for you, but it engulfs the world in this era. There are two options available for you. One is for you to be silent and tolerate the pain, and the other is that you can protest and prove that you're superior to others. To show your strength by fighting, and to fight, you must know the art of weapons.'

'What is a weapon, Guruji?' asked Aryan.

'A weapon is anything that can be used to strike and hurt someone. You can say even this stick is a weapon,' Swamiji replied.

'What are the uses of a weapon?'

'Like everything, a weapon has its pros and cons. A weapon can give you victory, but it can also destroy your conscience. It's up to you how you use it.'

Swami Brahmanand marked the question in his eyes. He continued, 'Right now, you needn't know about all this. All you need to know is how to handle different kinds of weapons, their working and use.'

Aryan nodded.

'Aryan, now you are eleven years old. You have practised yoga with deep concentration, and now it will be very helpful for your new lessons. You need to know and follow some rules before going through your new lessons. Come with me.'

Swamiji moved to the Natraj idol, where he offered his regular prayers. Aryan followed him and was stunned on seeing the idol.

'Guruji, what's this?'

'This is an idol of Natraj, a form of Lord Shiva. This is the very place where I accepted you as my disciple when you were just a baby, and your journey towards your destiny began.'

'Lord Shiva and Natraj are the same, Guruji?'

'Yes.'

As the days passed, Aryan's questions gained depth.

'Guruji, how many gods are there?'

'God is the universal master; He is one and all.'

'Then why do we worship different gods, with different names and different mantras?'

'Aryan, can you see that mango tree over there, the jackfruit and many others? How do you distinguish between all of them? Though all of them are fruits, how do you differentiate them between?'

'By their taste and form. Although they are all fruits, they are different in appearance and size.'

'Exactly. In the same manner, the universal master has undergone many forms for different purposes. The Supreme is formless; He takes on various forms for different people, different religions. But the reality is that God is one; humanity is the true faith, and the religion of the soul is compassion.'

Aryan was listening with great concentration.

'The dawn is approaching. Now we should move on to the cave. Aryan, this weapon is related to your history, you must master your handling of this.' Swamiji showed him a sword,

Aryan was being trained in every weapon, and due to his flexible body, he performed better than other children of his age might have done. Aryan would practice when he didn't feel like sleeping. Alishan saw him practisingskilfully, and knew that her husband's skills had been born in him.

There was a target of a diamond, placed inside a circular glass coating, hanging from a long rope. It was moving in a circular fashion and somewhere near the circumference, the diamond was placed along with water bubbles. It was confusing to focus on, as the sun rays were getting reflected in the circular glass.

Flavius drew his curved bow and took a shot at the glass. The S-shaped arrow pierced the round glass, and it stopped moving. Syombhu Murthy noticed that it was the exact point where the diamond was placed.

'You are a real warrior, my son; you passed the first test. Now let's check your other skills. Forget that you are going to fight with the girl's father. Treat me as your competitor.'

'Accepted.' Flavius nodded in pride.

They started playing with bows and arrows in a bid to prove their skills and to win over the other. Alishan was afraid for her old father. But she was silent and hoped for him to win. The game went on for more than an hour and Flavius hit the old man, shooting an arrow in his leg that made the old man fall.

Alishan came running, shouting in anger, 'If you killed my father, I will make you pay!'

'Stop, my child!' Murthy called. 'He has proven to be the real warrior and all a father wants is to give the hand of his daughter to a real man who can protect her. One who respects and accepts all challenges without fear and who admires his daughter and showers love on her. He has all those attributes. I have been looking for a man just like this for you.'

Flavius pulled the arrow from his leg and tore a piece of cloth from his clothes and wrapped it around her father's leg to stop the bleeding. Alishan stared at the man, trying to see the person her father had seen.

Alishan felt bad, thinking of her first meeting with her husband and how her father had approved of their marriage. She closed her eyes and fell asleep near her son.

The next morning, Aryan started showing his skills to Swamiji. Swamiji smiled in satisfaction. He could see that Aryan would be the greatest warrior of his time.

'Never use your weapons on the powerless. Use your skills for your own protection, the protection of your dear ones and anybody who needs you. You must be generous and kind to everyone in your behaviour, in your attitude, which will define you in history.'

'From whom should I protect people, Guruji?'

'The time has not yet come. Just keep in mind that beyond this cave, there are dangerous animals, who don't have a conscience to distinguish between the bad and the good. They love to attack and harm others. In such a scenario, you have to show your strength. It's believed a weapon can't kill any animal; it's the manifestation of your decision that kills the animal. So, based on the situation, your decision will order this physical weapon to act accordingly.'

Aryan practised hard. The features of an adult had started appearing in Aryan. He was turning fifteen. The inquisitiveness of his mind had grown. Sometimes he got distracted, thinking of all the unanswered questions he still had. He sometimes asked Alishan, 'Maa, I have a question. Guruji and I look alike, but you seem different. Why?'

Alishan always ignored the question and asked him to ask Swamiji.

One day while practising Aryan performed very poorly.

'Aryan, what's the matter? Why is your performance not satisfactory today? I think your mind is somewhere else. I cannot tolerate this,' Swamiji said, annoyed.

'Guruji, a question has risen in my mind, and it has been troubling me for a few days. May I ask you?' Aryan asked politely.

Swamiji was silent for some time and then raised his eyebrows. 'You may,' he murmured.

'My body is changing, and hair is growing everywhere. Why is it so?'

'You were a child, and now you are growing up. Did you see this tree when it was a small plant?'

'Yes, Guruji' Aryan moved his gaze towards the tree and replied.

'Do you notice any change?'

'Guruji a few years back, when it was a plant, it was short in height, weaker, thin and bore very few leaves. Now it has grown taller, stronger, thicker and countless leaves cover it.'

'Similarly, you are growing up and your body is changing. I'm older than you, so I have even more changes. You understand?'

91

Aryan marked the changes and asked again, 'Guruji, your appearance and my appearance are similar. But Maa is very different. Why is that so?'

'Because your mother is a lady and we are men. The Almighty has created all creatures in pairs. Your mother, you and I are categorised as humans. For now, this much is enough, other related things. You must know the difference between a lady and a man.' The last line Swami Brahmanand whispered to himself.

The questions in Aryan's mind, regarding biology and life, were answered by Swamiji with very generic examples and with the help of sacred books.

Swami talked of the four Vedas, the Rig, Sam, Yajur and Atharva. Along with that, he spoke of the essence of life, giving examples from the Puranas, Upanishads and Bhagwat Gita.

'Why are these so important, how will they help me?' asked Aryan.

'All the words prescribed in these books are the words of the Creator. These are the means of life. For the wellbeing of humankind, He gifted us these words to teach us what life is, what its objective is...'

'What is life?'

'Life is just an illusion.'

'Then what is the real aspect of this world?'

'Death! Death is the ultimate truth. The Almighty is real, and nothing else. Everyone is here for a purpose! You must know what you are here for. But before that, you must learn the difference between good and evil.'

'How can I distinguish good from evil?'

'Both are inside you, inside all of us,' answered Swamiji.

'What is the difference?'

'Good is the voice of the Almighty, who guides you on the right path. He resides in the heart and controls the mind. But evil lies in the sense organs that guide you on the wrong path and if it controls your mind then you become a devil.'

'Where can I find the right and wrong path? How can I differentiate?' Aryan exclaimed.

14. Truth Weighs over Ignorance

'Observe the burning lamp. The truth is a burning lamp; it will throw light in the direction that your life is meant to tread. But if you look below the lamp, the dark shadow can be observed that speaks one more truth. If you want to choose the opposite side of truth, you will be trapped in the circular shadow throughout your life out of ignorance, and your path will never lead to your destiny. The *Bhagwat Gita* says, out of compassion for them, I, dwelling in their hearts, destroy, with the shining lamp of knowledge the darkness born of ignorance.'

'How can we destroy ignorance, Guruji?'

'By self-realization, by controlling our mind. Our mind is like a running horse; we should know how to control it. We should allow our conscience to speak, rather than our mind. Our conscience, our inner soul knows for what we exist on this earth.' The completely naked man spoke the truth of life, standing in front of Aryan. No one else was there when he was teaching the child the essence of life. Both wore nothing but human flesh. The mother kept herself hidden behind the bushes, keeping her promise, and allowing the child to grow into a man under Swamiji's supervision.

Swamiji moved on, and Aryan followed him with a confused mind. Swami Brahmanand led him to a dark cave, where a strange scene amazed and shocked Aryan. A medium-sized stone covered the mouth of the cave. Bushes around the stone made it impossible to conceive of any opening. When the stone was pulled aside and they descended, Aryan saw that there were openings cut into the cave to allow light to filter inside. They were designs on the walls, depicting rituals, and many figures of prominent people. An enormous black stone, hanging by a thin thread, was swinging to and fro like a pendulum, while a peacock feather hanging from a similar thread was stable.

Swamiji asked, 'Do you understand what you see in front of you?'

Aryan was quite astonished. He glared at both the objects.

'It's a miracle. A huge stone shouldn't move, it should be stable as per nature and the feather, the light weight object, should swing. Why is it this way, Guruji?'

'The big stone is a symbol of evil, and the feather is a symbol of peace, a symbol of love. Evil minds are all over the world, distributed in an uneven fashion. There is no stability of mind, thoughts or work. But still they exist, to help us to distinguish between right and wrong, the dawn and the dusk, to bring to light the existence of the truth. The feather is the symbol of an extraordinary man looking for peace, establishing love, and if required, fighting for the right. The path is destined for him and the rays are clearly visible, so there is no disturbing movement seen, and there is no distraction,' said the sage, looking at the astonishing scene before them.

Swamiji's voice was heavy and his words were inspiring for the child, and the nuances of life were interesting for him to learn. Before going through the spiritual books, Swami Brahmanand always presented before him some detailed example to learn from.

Once Aryan's capabilities and appetite for knowledge stoked Swamiji's confidence in him, Swamiji ordered him to read the books inside the cave before the dawn and to practice his weapon after dusk.

The devoted disciple followed Swamiji's words. He would read the books of myths, the Bhagawat Gita and other Puranas, in the absence of Swamiji. When he read, he learned about the three paths to salvation: karma yoga, jnana yoga and bhakti yoga.

In karma yoga, Lord Krishna talks about Dharma as one's personal duty by saying, 'Now if you do not execute this battle, then having given up your dharma, you shall incur sin.'

Arjuna argued that if he and Krishna were to fight the Battle of Kurukshetra, they would be treading the path of adharma and committing sin. To which Lord Krishna told Arjuna, who was heartbroken by seeing his near and dear ones on the battlefield, that 'the truth is quite contrary. In war, there is no place for emotions, the only truth that stands is to do or die.' Aryan was reading aloud, turning the pages of the book one by one.

'In war, there is no place for emotions… The only truth that stands is to do or die,' Alishan whispered the truth to herself. She turned back, as she did not wish to cry in front of her child. The flashback of yesteryears was clearly in front of her. Because of his emotions, Flavius had been defeated in his last battle.

tasmātsarveṣukāleṣu

māmanusmarayudhyaca

mayyarpita-mano-buddhir

96

māmevaiṣyasyasaṁśayaḥ

Aryan chanted the mantra, the way he had been taught by his guru.

'Our love is growing, my love. If you were here, you would have been happy, seeing him growing like a warrior,' whispered Alishan to herself, her eyes moist as she thought of her husband.

Alishanwas distracted by the tiger's roar. As the dusk arrived with Swamiji, he called out for Aryan, who was reading the sacred books. Aryan got up and went to Swamiji. Swamiji put his hands on Aryan's shoulders and said, 'Aryan, today is a very auspicious day. It's a perfect day, as even after the sun sets the light will remain. So today I'm going to give you a new lesson, a lesson of love, a lesson of care... a lesson of bonding...'

Swamiji was moving towards the centre of the thick forest, far away from the cave. Aryan followed him silently with folded hands. He was enjoying his first walk in the light without the fear of the sun as it had set.

Swamiji closed his eyes and stood still for some time. Opening his eyes and raising his hands towards his mouth, he started imitating certain birds and animals' voices, one by one. The forest started responding. Soon there was a huge gathering surrounding them, several types of birds and animals. Aryan turned around, took stock of the gathering; he had never seen such a variety of birds and animals before. Some of the birds were singing and moving around Swamiji, and few of them sat on Swamiji's hand as he raised it. It seemed, the birds were interacting with Swamiji, and he was responding. Brushing his fingers over a bird's head, Swamiji spoke, 'I can see that you want to ask something. Let me clarify before you ask... As I said before, today's is a special class for you... love, mercy, care and bonding is the theme.'

Aryan was listening very carefully to each and every word from Swamiji. As he was elaborating upon the idea of love, a jingling sound distracted Aryan. A fresh breeze carrying flowery essence started flowing and the jingling sound came again. Aryan's eyes began searching for the origin.

'Aryan, what are you looking for?'

'Guruji, I heard some sound that I have heard never before.'

'Concentrate on my words. No such sound is audible to me.'

Swamiji continued his lesson on love, the need for love of nature. The trees, birds, and animals, everyone needed to be loved and cared for. This love gradually increases the bond between humans and nature. This bond had helped Swamiji gain the power to interact with nature.

'If you love them, in return they will love you too. If you care for them, they will help you. If you harm them, they will kill you. This is the law of nature. Even the legendary epic tells us to follow the law of nature. Hence from today, you need to feel love of nature and learn how to interact with it. There is no particular language of love. Observation is the best language.'

Swamiji started to train Aryan in the language of birds and animals. Though difficult for an ordinary human, Aryan picked up on the lessons quickly. It was now getting darker, but Aryan was involved and quite lost in learning. As the moon shone with all its cool white light, the 'Chham… chham' echo distracted Aryan again.

Aryan closed his eyes to meditate, as all these days of training, Swamiji had instructed him to do so whenever he got distracted.

15. Mirage Shines in the Dark

Pretty little feet, garlanded with silver anklets, were hurrying on the road, serenading with 'Chham…chham'. The long gown with golden embroidery was pulled up to keep her from toppling down while running.

A strand of her hair, decorated with flowers and shining beads, was swinging to and fro, kissing her face. A smile played on her red lips, and her shining eyes brimmed with joy.

Terrifying lightning began piercing the dark sky along with high winds. The inhabitants of Kumbhgarh who were strolling on the street ran to their houses. A donkey was braying loudly, raising its head. Traders thronged the city. Some traders, unable to control their horses, fell off and ran to a source of shelter. Big drops followed the harsh wind. The girl took refuge in a broken temple. Darkness engulfed the temple, which was far from any houses. People were surprised to see the dark temple glowing with light.

There was a belief that this girl visited the temple and was welcomed with open doors. But no one knew more than that. The belief was that, whenever she entered the temple, it wrought havoc, and the weather turned stormy. It was a bad omen.

'Looks like the big iron-locker has opened on its own, as the bell has started clinking. The peculiar sound of the black crows says something bad has happened or is going to happen soon,' said a young man.

'Time may unfold the mystery of this young princess. Though her mother was a spiritual soul, no one knows what this darkness is hidden in the temple...'

Inside the temple, the princess was moving around, casting a shadow on the wall with the light of a small candle placed at the centre, on the statue of a bull.

'Maa... I'm here Maa...'

Tears were rolling from the girl's eyes, but she seemed content. She was waiting for her mother in the lonely place. A soft and delicate hand came from behind and wiped away her tears. The princess turned with a smiling face and hugged her mother tightly. Seliana was overjoyed to see her daughter.

'Maa, I wait for this day every year to meet you. Why, why can't we meet every day?' Ritwi sobbed.

'Sweetheart, it's my fate and yours. We are bound to wait for your birthday every year. Let me look at you, my doll. When I was with you, I never allowed you to move out of my sight. But now for a ten years, crying every day and waiting to meet you on your birthday has been my pitiful life. Tell me how you are? Is everything alright with you?'

'I'm fine Maa, but these last few days, I have spent many sleepless nights. Sometimes I feel restless, and I don't know the reason.'

Seliana closed her eyes and folded her hands, facing the Shiv-Ling.

'How is your father? I hope he takes good care of you?'

'Yes, Maa. He is fine, he cares for me more than anything, but he has been out of the city for the last ten days on work. He will probably arrive today; he had promised to be here before dusk. He should be on his way home.'

'So be it…' Seliana whispered to self.

'Maa, I want to take a nap in your lap,' Ritwi said like a small child.

Seliana smiled and brushed her hands over the princess's head and nodded in approval. She settled herself beside a pillar, and Ritwi lay down, putting her head in her lap. Seliana continued brushing her hand over the girl's head and forehead. The girl pulled her other hand close to her lips and kissed it and closed her eyes.

On the dark stormy night, bullock carts and horse carriages were moving on a twisted and curled path up in the hills. Guards accompanied a caravan, walking beside it. As they entered a narrow road, bandits attacked suddenly. The bandits outnumbered the guards. Armed with sharp weapons, the thieves started slaying the guards. After taking over the carts, the bandit group headed towards the horse carriage.

'Hey trader, come out. All of your guards have been dispatched. Now it's your turn!'

'What do you want?' asked the trader from inside the carriage.

'We want all your prosperity… haha…' one of the bandits said.

'You already have all my bullock carts. Let me go.'

101

'Oh, do you think that we will leave you?' The leader laughed. 'The real treasure is with you. Give it to us and then we will leave you.'

Two bandits came to the leader and said, 'Sardar, the carts are empty. It seems he was on a trading mission.'

'Bring him out!' the Sardar ordered.

Faces lost their outlines in the darkness and only a silhouette suggested that the stout tradesman was carrying a bag. The bandits began breaking the carriage into pieces. Holding the tradesman, the robbers snatched his bag and turned it upside down, making the gold and silver coins fall on the ground. As the bandit leader raised his sword to behead the man, a few boys in their late teens jumped from a nearby stone, pushing the tradesman aside. The boys were armed. Though few in number, they proved to be efficient in the fight. They obstructed the bandit's attack flawlessly, and the fight lasted for some time. The boys' leader gave priority to saving the lives of those they had come to protect. But with time, fatigue took over and most of them grew exhausted from lost blood. However, the young leader showed no sign of fatigue; he prevented every attack flawlessly, and this infused energy in the other fighters.

The stormy night was coming to an end, but the fight continued. While the red horizon signalled dawn, one of the bandits announced that the villagers were marching towards them with sticks and Sardar ordered his group to leave. Just before leaving, the ferocious, powerful strike from bandit Sardar injured the young leader severely.

A young boy who had left the group to summon aid came running, shouting, 'Crystal! Don't worry, the villagers are here.'

By the time people had arrived the bandits had left and vanished into the mountains. The villagers helped the injured onto the bullock carts.

'Are you alright? Where are you from? Don't you know this path isn't safe at night?' a villager asked the tradesman.

'I'm Mathews, Chief of the Eastern Zone. Are the fighters alright?'

'They need some medical attention; they all seem to be exhausted,' a villager replied.

'Help them, please, they saved my life. I wish to felicitate them in a grand way, especially the brave boy, Crystal.'

'As you wish,' the villagers said, and drove the carts to the Chief's city.

Once there, servants guided everyone to the guests' section of the palace at the Chief's order. Ritwi was peeping out of the window. As soon as she saw her father heading towards the entrance, she moved away.

The Vaidya had been called as soon as the party entered in the palace and aid was being given to everyone. Chief Mathews strolled through the rooms, taking stock of the condition of every fighter. Ritwi came into the chamber.

'Father, are you alright?'

'I am, but these fighters need some help. They have saved your father's life from the bandits,' Chief said.

Crystal has been unconscious but as soon as Ritwi entered and he heard her voice, the Vaidya noticed some movement in his hand.

'I've given the required treatment to everyone. They are all are in good condition, but this boy needs a bit more care,' he said, pointing to Crystal.

Ritwi turned towards him and Crystal opened his eyes. They looked directly into each other's eyes. Ritwi moved her gaze towards the Vaidya, but Crystal's eyes were stuck on Ritwi. She stole a sight of Crystal from the corners of her eyes, and when she realized that Crystal was staring at her, she felt electrified, and looked away.

Feeling that Ritwi was uncomfortable, Crystal got up from the bed. Seeing this, the Vaidya asked him not to move and take rest until complete recovery, but Crystal chose to ignore him.

'I should leave sir... I'm feeling much better now.' Saying this, Crystal moved but his legs got twisted, and he stumbled to the floor.

'Young man, you need rest, and must recover from your sprain. After all, you are deserving of extraordinary hospitality and care because you and your team saved my life,' Chief said, holding Crystal's hand and helping him back to bed.

Hearing this, Ritwi's attention became focused on Crystal. There was respect for him in her eyes. Crystal even marked this reaction and accepted the proposal to stay in the palace.

As the days passed, Crystal recovered slowly. Ritwi personally monitored the treatment of the saviour of her father. When the medicine was being administered to Crystal's manly body, Ritwi's would get distracted every time. She was attracted to Crystal in some way. She had already reached the age at which she had begun paying attention to boys. If help were required, and there were no one else present, Ritwi managed the situation. The Vaidya was happy with the boy's progress.

'You are a strong man indeed. The other day, Chief was telling us how magnificently you obstructed the bandits' attack and saved his life. Chief is very obliged to you for your act of valour,' the old Vaidya said.

'Vaidyaji, I'm happy that I could save his life and property. My fluency in the art of weapons has been useful,' said Crystal. 'Perhaps that fight has been the inception of my life's destiny,' he said, and smiled at Ritwi.

Just then Chief entered.

'So young man, are you feeling well? Is there anything I can get you...?'

'No sir, I'm perfectly fine. I am grateful for your hospitality. I'm not equal to you, but you have cared for me. I'm honoured.'

'No, young man. Status isn't defined by money or assets. You have defined your own status with your bravery by saving my life,' Chief said, patting Crystal's shoulder.

'To my honour, you have justified my status. Since I have completely recovered, I seek your permission to take leave,' Crystal said politely.

'I can accept your request on one condition. You have to accept my offer...'

Crystal couldn't figure out what offer Chief was talking about. He looked confusedly at the Chief.

Chief chuckled and said, 'My offer is that you accept the position of the lead fighter in my kingdom. You can meet your parents and come back...'

'I could have accepted the proposal with grace but sir, I can't make any promise about this. I've never left my parents, and I owe them everything. They can't live without me, and I can't leave them.'

'Beautiful! Then you can bring your parents with you, this way you can satisfy me as well as your parents!'

'I require their acceptance first. If they accept this, I won't have any objections'

'I hope they accept it.' Giving a touch of arrogance to his moustache Chief said.

Crystal peeped behind Chief at Ritwi, who was standing silently. Then he moved towards the door.

'Wait a moment, brave man!' Chief called out. 'I owe you for saving my life. Please accept this.' Saying this, Chief gave him a cloth bag full of gold coins.

'Thank you, sir, but I don't need this. I did not save your life for money…'

'Splendid thought, but I want to give you something. What can I give you? Just ask. Ask me for anything you want. I will give it to you wholeheartedly.'

Crystal smiled and glanced at Ritwi. 'Sir, I don't need anything as of now. Perhaps I will demand something later.'

'Anytime, young man. Whenever you demand and whatever it may be, I will not let you down.'

Crystal left the palace compound with his friends and Ritwi went to her room. Chief was standing at the entrance and brushing his moustache with his finger tips.

16. Enticed by Love

On a white piece of cloth, a hand strove to do a sketch using a handmade brush and charcoal paste. The eyes opened on the piece of fabric, followed by a sharp nose and then by lips. It seemed like significant efforts had been put into defining the lips. The sketch appeared to be that of a beautiful girl. The brush rolled down to her shoulder. The swinging curls looked as though the wind were blowing them smoothly from behind. As soon as the sketch was done, smiling lips came closer and kissed the forehead of this creation. The smiling lips belong to Crystal, who was trying to sketch Ritwi's countenance on the piece of cloth.

Crystal seemed satisfied with his creation. He held the sketch in both hands, too close, as if he wanted her to come alive. Just then, an eagle woke him from his fantasy as it settled on his hands.

'Jewel…do you know this girl in my hands?'

Jewel fluttered her wings and looked at the sketch.

'She is the love of my life. I have never seen a girl like her and I do not even expect to see one in my dreams.' Crystal spoke slowly, as if beguiled by Ritwi's beauty.

'Ritwi, when I felt the first tender touch of your hands, I was taken to some other world where it was just the two of us. I saw roaring waterfalls, the dense forest...'

'Crystal!' A feminine voice distracted Crystal from his fantasy world.

'Jewel, is Maa looking for me?' Crystal asked the eagle. The eagle responded by fluttering its wings, and raised its body in the air. Crystal hid the sketch in a tree branch and followed the voice, picking up his sword which was lying on the stone.

The next day, Crystal returned to the tree in which he had hidden the sketch and searched for it. He searched all over but unable to find it. He looked through the surroundings, hoping that it might have slipped off the branch, but he found no trace of it. The thought of losing Ritwi's sketch made him nervous. Crystal whispered to himself, 'What if someone finds it? It may bring him trouble.' Then he consoled himself by telling himself that no one would recognize her in the sketch.

With mixed thoughts, he flumped on the stone, took out another piece of cloth and started writing a poem of love. He closed his eyes imagining Ritwi as he wrote about her beauty, the curve of a smile on his lips. Soon, the piece of cloth was impregnated with Ritwi's beauty. Every single word unveiled his love for Ritwi, and the fabric reflected intense love.

This became a routine. He would come to the same place, and express his love either in writing or through sketches, but whenever he hid the piece of cloth, he could not find it again. But Crystal was so enamoured of his love that this scarcely bothered him.

Ritwi was playing with a rabbit in her room, caressing it. Suddenly, another rabbit rushed from the balcony towards her. The panicked movement surprised Ritwi. She went to the balcony to perceive the reason behind it. She searched all over but she could not find anything suspicious. Suddenly, high up in the air some crows cawed restlessly. She looked up to see an eagle in flight. It soared close and settled on the balcony. It fluttered its wings before resting and looking at Ritwi.

Ritwi was petrified to see a big eagle at an arm's distance. She stepped back slowly and her hands searched for things with which to threaten the eagle. She found a vase, and lifted it. Just as she was about to throw it at the eagle, it flew away.

Ritwi put the vase back in its place and anxiously peeped out to make sure that the eagle had gone. She saw the big bird fluttering its wings and moving high in the air, and the small crows chasing it. Ritwi relaxed and was about to go inside, but her eyes saw a folded piece of cloth on the balcony floor. She picked up and unfolded it very carefully, walking inside her room.

Her eyes widened, and her lips parted in shock.

'Oh god, what's this? Is this a piece of glass! Do I see my reflection?' Ritwi blabbered in excitement. The cloth held a beautiful sketch of Ritwi.

'I wonder who made this? It is so perfect and more beautiful than I am. Where did this come from? Did someone throw it up? But this cloth is very light, and it would be almost impossible for anyone to throw it to this height.' She was so mesmerised by the picture that she did not blink her eyes for a long time. Yes! She was in love with herself.

Some other day, Ritwi was humming a tune while standing on her balcony. The melody seemed to be echoing her loneliness. Just then she was distracted by a loud fluttering at her back. As she moved her eyes towards the sound, she was horrified to see the eagle again. She tried to find some tool with which to threaten the eagle but couldn't find any, and she didn't dare to step into her room. The eagle turned its back to Ritwi after a while and flew away but while taking off, it dropped a piece of cloth, and Ritwi noticed it.

Ritwi picked it up but this time, she unfolded it quickly and anxiously, expecting a sketch as she had received earlier. This time she found a poem. She closed all the doors of her room and sat on the bed. She started reading the lines but stopped for a moment and re-read it from the beginning.

The beauty of your eyes says that...

My love resides in the corner of your heart

Maybe your smile is a reflection of my art

But I am tired of the steps to your heart...

Like the sky, waiting for its stars...

I will wait for those magic moments

When for love the nature mends

And the sands of the time will tell the tale of ours...

She could feel the beauty of every word reflecting the immense love of the poet. With her eyes closed, she traveled to her dream world. She was standing lonely in a dense forest with waterfalls at a distance. She bent near a pond and glanced at her reflection. She had never admired her beauty like this before; she had never praised herself before. She adored the charms that were described in the poem. All of a sudden, hoofbeats drew her away from her magic world. She followed the direction of the sound and saw a boy riding a horse. The rider had long black hair flowing swiftly with the wind. She tried to concentrate on the rider's face but couldn't make it out. She rubbed her eyes for clear vision but in vain, as the rider stopped at a distance.

'Do I know you? Do you know me? What's your name?' Ritwi asked.

The rider was silent, and he pulled the reins back. With this, the horse raised its forelegs and moved on.

'Wait, I need to talk to you…know you…!'

The rider glanced at her and threw back a bunch of roses. As the flowers were falling, the rider sped up and vanished. Ritwi stepped on a rose and its thorns pierced her foot, causing her to scream in pain. She woke up in panic, then realized it was a dream.

The next day, Ritwi was trying to give her vision of the rider shape on canvas, standing on her balcony. She had drawn the horse and the rider's outline, but without any detailing of the face, as she was unable to see it in her dreams. While she was moving her hands over the sketch, a cold breeze caressed her, and she closed her eyes. She tried to sense the breeze. Suddenly, she heard the distant sound of hooves. She turned towards the sound, but there was no one there. She smiled mischievously at her own madness and resumed her work, but her eyes once again turned to the road below. She could now see a young man riding a horse. Ritwi rested her hands on the railing of the balcony and focused on the man. The silhouette of the horse and rider was same as that in her sketch. Ritwi tried to concentrate on him.

'Do I know him? It seems we have met earlier. Yes! He is the same boy! My father's saviour.'

The rider raised his eyes to steal a glance of Ritwi, who was standing on the balcony of her room. Ritwi was still trying to see Crystal's gestures and harmonise them with her sketch. Many of the features seemed to match. Suddenly, the eagle approached the balcony and fluttered its wings. Ritwi anxiously looked to find a gift from the unknown admirer, but today there was nothing. The eagle flew over the rider and soon as the rider stopped, the eagle perched on his shoulder. Seeing this, Ritwi was dumbstruck.

'Welcome, Crystal, my savior!' Chief Mathews exclaimed.

'I'm honoured, Chief.'

'So Crystal, what brings you here after such a long time?' Chief asked, putting his hands on Crystal's shoulder. They entered the palace. Ritwi moved back to her room.

Chief and Crystal seated themselves. Chief clapped thrice and within moments a man entered the room with a jug full of wine and two glasses. He poured the wine into the glasses. Chief handed one to Crystal.

'Have some; this will make you feel relaxed.'

Crystal hesitated, 'No sir, I can't.'

'Why? You are old enough to have it. Your powers will be enhanced, this is the best wine available in the country and expensive too. Don't feel shy, enjoy it.'

'No Chief, I'm thankful for your offer, but I can't have this in front of you as you are of the age of my father.'

'Oho...respect! Good. But I give you the freedom to enjoy and by the way, what about my other offer--did you discuss it?' saying this, Chief quaffed all the wine in his glass.

'Yes Chief, I'm here to announce my acceptance of the proposal.'

'Incredible'.

'But I have some conditions.'

'As you wish, brave boy.'

'My parents will have to stay with me.'

'That's fine, boy. I'm desperate to meet the parents of a brave boy like you.'

'That is all, Chief. I will take **your** leave now.'

'Wait a moment, boy.' Chief stood up. 'What about the gift that I owe you? You can ask me for anything you want.'

'The appropriate time hasn't yet arrived. I will ask when it comes.'

'Well done my boy, I was expecting an answer like this. You justify my decision in choosing you. You and your family need not worry; I will personally look into the arrangements for you.'

'May I leave now, Chief?'

'Come back soon with your family. My city is eagerly waiting to witness your velour.'

Crystal moved out of the palace and saddled his horse, but his eyes were searching for Ritwi. As the horse began to march forward, Crystal looked behind, hoping on a call to wait.

'A moment, please! Sir!'

It was Ritwi'smaid calling out to Crystal. He stopped, and his eyes went towards the entrance where Ritwi was standing. Crystal hopped down from the horse and Ritwi moved towards him.

'Are you alright?' Ritwi inquired.

'Yes, and you?'

'What does that mean? I'm always fine, and I asked about you because you were injured.'

'Oh...I mistook your question, I'm sorry.'

Jewel was perched on Crystal's shoulder.

'This eagle, is it your pet?'

'She has grown up with me as my friend. Her name is Jewel.'

Ritwi clapped twice and her maid came forward. Ritwi whispered something in her ears, and the maid nodded while listening attentively. The maid moved back to the palace after taking her orders. Ritwi asked Crystal to walk with her in the garden, and Crystal followed.

'So what was your name? Let me remember... yes, Crystal. What do you do apart from fighting and saving lives?'

'Is this some kind of a joke?'

'No I just want to know you, learn about your hobbies, likes and dislikes. The last interaction we had was not very informative.'

'I love to paint. I'm fond of art, literature and weapons,' was all Crystal could say.

'Then you must have a soft corner in the core of your brave heart...'

'Perhaps.'

The maid approached with something that was wrapped in a red cloth. She handed it to Ritwi and then left.

'What's this?' Crystal inquired.

'This is something that I need to know from you.'

Crystal was clueless. Ritwi unwrapped the red cloth. Inside there were white cloth pieces. Crystal was getting anxious. Ritwi unfolded the cloth pieces and spread them on the grass. The first was her sketch, then the poem and then one after another, more poems and sketches emerged. Crystal was embarrassed at seeing his missing paintings and sketches laid out in front of the girl who had been an inspiration to those crafts!

'Do you know who owns them?' Ritwi asked Crystal.

'Where did you get them?'

'So you do know who made them.'

'It was me, but how did they reach you?'

'Your childhood friend would deliver them to my balcony.'

'Oh, I'm sorry! Believe me; I did not intend to send them to you…I had just made them for my…'

'Oh, is that so! Then the bird came to me without your knowledge? Why did you make them?'

At first Crystal was shy, and then he decided to come clean.

'I've poured out my feelings for you, and you can accept or reject them as you see fit. But I'm in love with you, and have been from the day we first met.'

115

'I know. Your work has demonstrated that.'

'So…'

'So what?'

'Your reply?'

'You know, when I saw your creations I was confused at first. Each of your creations presented a more beautiful side of me to myself, making me fall in love with myself again and again. Your emotions are so well expressed in each of these pieces that I was mesmerised by the touch of love. I experienced a new world of dreams in which I'm caressed and loved more than anything else.'

Taking the initiative, Crystal wrapped his arm around Ritwi's waist and pulled her close. It was a whole new experience for Ritwi, but she didn't resist. She submitted at the moment and closed her eyes. Crystal lowered his face towards Ritwi's to plant a kiss on her quivering lips, but as soon as she felt the warm breaths on her face, she moved her face away, opening her eyes.

'Why are you moving? I love you, and you love me, then why this hesitation? It is a token of our love.'

'Crystal, I haven't decided on you. I love the way you love me and the way you expressed it.'

'Then why this response?'

'Maybe I need some time…' Ritwi replied.

17. Confronting a New World! Alone!

The training of Aryan was going smoothly. Aryan was soaking in all the tips and information Swamiji gave him. Aryan had acquired the knowledge to interact with nature. He was now able to talk and share his feelings with the animals and birds living in the forest. With age, his powers and control improved.

Swamiji taught him the secrets of handling weapons flawlessly and guided him on the situations in which weapons should be used.

Then there was the big responsibility of magic. Magic needs to be practiced with wise hands. If acquired by evil, then it may prove to be the most destructive thing in the world. But Swamiji had no issues with sharing his magical insights with Aryan. He was brought up wisely under the guidance of Swamiji and his loving mother, Alishan.

'Aryan, magic is not for selfish use. You need to use it for others for a good cause, and never grow arrogant because of the powers you acquire. You must use it with humility. For now, you can't learn the powers of magic until you turn twenty-one. Right now you should concentrate on form, tricks and the right time for the use of magic.'

Swamiji taught him the art of magic but ordered him not to use it for personal gains. A human who had the potential to handle the power of magic could not misuse it else it would become the reason for his self-destruction in the future. Swamiji taught him how important it was to wait for the right time to use magic, or else it would become ineffective.

'How long will I have to wait to use it efficiently?'

'Your destiny will decide that for you. You'll know when you are capable enough to use it. Until then, you'll have to be patient.'

After teaching him magic tricks, Swamiji had no more to teach Aryan, as he has shared all of his knowledge. Swamiji decided to depart from the forest, leaving Aryan and Alishan behind.

'Aryan, I have shared with you all my knowledge and you have never given me cause to complain. You have completed your training. Now, you are almost ready for life. You are powered with the lessons you have learned, but you have to wait for some days before that knowledge bears fruit in your favour.'

'This has been made possible by your blessings Guruji. Under your guidance, I have achieved many things that were impossible otherwise. I owe you my life Guruji. What's next for me, Guruji?'

'Aryan, I will be leaving this forest soon. I want you to obey every order of your mother.'

'I should not ask this Guruji, but I have an urge to know more about this decision of yours.'

'Nothing is constant and everlasting in this world, my child. Everyone is a guest in this world, each one comes with an assigned role, and completion of the work must be our primary motive. After completion, one's role and existence come to an end and so mine has.

I had a major duty to fulfill, and that was to train you and make you capable of facing your destiny. As my responsibility is done, I have to leave. Don't think about your destiny, because it will come to you eventually. Your training will help you once I leave. Continue your practice by yourself and try perfecting your skills as much as you can.'

Aryan was silent. He was not satisfied with Guruji's answer. He was confused about his wellbeing and his fate that was yet to unfold.

'Aryan, grant me one last promise before I leave.'

'Guruji, as you say.'

'Never venture into sunlight, not until your mother permits you to do so. Remember all my teachings until your death, never be rude to anyone and destroy evil with the powers you have earned throughout your life.'

Aryan bent down on his knees and touched Swamiji's feet. He said, 'I promise Guruji…I will follow each and every word as directed by you without any excuse.'

'Aryan, we have a tradition of Guru Dakshina which the disciple owes to the Guru. The disciple has to give whatever is demanded by the guru, and even you will have to do the same.'

'Guruji, I don't own anything. Everything is yours. You have made me what I am. What can I give you? I am all yours, and without you I'm nothing.'

Guruji smiled at this answer. 'Aryan, I am pleased with your intelligent reply. I bless you to rule the world with wise motives.' He put his hand on Aryan's head, blessing him.

'But you have to give me my Guru Dakshina whenever I ask, no matter what it is. It is a tradition no one can be exempt from.'

'Certainly, Guruji…'

'Now move to the cave to your mother. The dawn has arrived. Tell her about my decision.'

Saying this, Guruji moved ahead, and didn't turn back even once. Aryan waited for some time with moist eyes. These tears showed his respect, dedication and love for Swamiji. Then he went towards the cave. As soon as he reached it, he informed his mother of Swamiji's decision. Alishan was stunned for a moment and then she ran out of the cave, pausing only to wrap her saree around herelf. She hurried to look for Swamiji. She called for him in the forest, trying to find him. Finally, after some time, she found Swamiji .Alishan ran and fell at his feet.

'Swamiji, why? I was under oath not to ask you but today I'm breaking my promise. Why are you leaving us? Who will guide us in this evil world? Who will protect us from evil powers?' Alishan was screaming in despair.

'Alishan, get up, don't panic. I have made Aryan powerful enough to face this cruel world with all the powers that I had.'

'But Swamiji, Aryan is just a child. How can he face the cruel world? He has not seen the world beyond this forest!'

'Aryan has grown up enough to face it all with mighty powers and dedication. A mother can't feel her child's growth. A child remains a child forever in his parents' eyes, so you have not noticed his growth.'

'Swamiji you had said that you are dedicated to this forest and won't ever leave it. So why this decision?'

'Alishan, in these few years I have committed a major sin, so I need to purify my body and soul. For that, I'm moving to my Lord's place which is a journey of three months. The day will come soon, the day when Aryan's fate will be decided. Aryan will face a tremendous trouble. I have to start my journey today so I can be back before that day arrives. I have to accumulate more powers for your child.'

'What sin, Swamiji?'

'I have remained nude for so many years, and religious words depict after taking 'Guru Mantra' we mustn't stay naked for whatever circumstances may be, that is a sin. Still, I have remained nude for several years. You need not panic. I have made Aryan promise to follow my directions. I'm leaving the tiger for your protection, stay calm and relaxed. I will be back.'

'But Swamiji, what will be the outcome of the trouble he will face?'

'Don't worry, victory will be yours as you and your child are on the right path.' Saying this, Swamiji vanished into the dense forest.

Alishan stared after him for some time, then while getting up, she picked up the sand from Swamiji's footprint and put it on her forehead. Then she moved back towards the cave.

Kumbhgarh, Ritwi's palace balcony.

Ritwi was sitting down, and Crystal was standing next to her. Their interaction and body language signified that they were quite close, and that they were at ease with one another. The wind was blowing, and Ritwi's hair fanned out slightly. Crystal helped her tie it back into a bun.

'Before you came here, I was a girl. The little girl in me used to dream of the man who would come into her life. But now I am afraid that I may see that dream fulfilled in you…'

'You don't have to fear for tomorrow…' Crystal replied.

Ritwi's face was cast down with shyness.

'Come with me. I'll prove to be the man of your dreams. I'll give pleasure this evening; you just need to trust me…' Crystal said.

'I think I need some more time. I am afraid of giving myself to you. I want a change; I want to explore life beyond this…' Ritwi said.

'If you want, I can help you. I can ask your father, and if he permits I can show you the world, I can help you explore the world beyond these walls…' Crystal said.

'No… I want to explore it alone. I don't want to be dependent on someone all my life. I am not a poor girl anymore. I am grown up, and I can choose my world. I hope you understand. Just give me some space and let me think about us…' Ritwi said.

Crystal nodded, agreeing with her and allowing her to think about their relationship. With a smile on his lips, he moved out of the room, saying, 'I'll wait for your decision. I hope you won't disappoint me. I love you.'

Ritwi was quite disturbed listening to Crystal. She was silent, and still.

18. Unfold the New World Beyond the Horizon

'Does the world end at the horizon? Have you seen what's beyond the sea?' Standing at a distance from the sea shore, Aryan was questioning the birds of Satwaparvat jungle in their language, but he didn't receive any detailed answer. He started swinging on the swing built of twigs and stared over the sea. Suddenly a small bird which was not able to fly well fell down from its nest onto Aryan's lap. Aryan caressed it with love and keeping the little one in his lap, he spoke in its language.

'Little one, how did you fall?'

The small bird replied, 'I want to fly up in the sky. I want to cross the sea and see the new world. There I will find many things and different types of food to feed on.'

'Little one, there is no new world behind the sea. It's just water and water,' said Aryan pampering the little bird.

'You don't know. My mother told me once that there are villages and

123

cities beyond the sea, where humans live. They are very knowledgeable and kind, they serve food to the birds, their food is not the fruits and seeds that we eat in this forest. They use fire to make food.'

Aryan was surprised by this reply. No one had ever told him of life beyond the sea. He was distracted from his thoughts by the small bird's voice. 'I'm just waiting for my wings to grow strong enough to fly for longer distances, so that I can cross the sea and discover the world that is waiting for me.'

The bird's mother came down from her nest and ordered her child to come back as it was growing dark. Aryan began to burn with impatience at not knowing what lay on the other side of the sea. He decided to head back to the cave and confront his mother about all she had kept from him.

'Why has this fact been kept hidden from me, Maa? You and Guruji have never allowed me to go beyond the marked boundary, why? I know that there is life beyond the sea, masses of humans reside there, and there are villages and cities as well.' Aryan spoke angrily.

Alishan was stunned when she heard this, but she gathered her strength and replied, 'Yes, what you now know is true, but things are different for you; you will come to know at the right time.'

'When will that right time come?' argued Aryan.

'Your Guruji will guide you beyond the sea when he returns from his pilgrimage; you have to be patient till then.'

'Why I have been denied this knowledge and why has my life always had limits?'

'Aryan, you are independent, all these secrets and restrictions are just precautionary measures for your safety. This is not the right time for you to know all. My son, you have to wait few more days.' Saying this, Alishan turned back towards the cave's entrance. Aryan wasn't satisfied with the answers given to him; he just looked towards his mother's retreating figure with helpless eyes.

From then on, he was in search of answers to the many questions boggling his mind. One evening, he took steps to a destination. He walked to the coast of the sea, looking at the tides.

'What the waves might bring and where the sea of thoughts might take you, you never know... There will never be an end to an illusion if there is no beginning. The sea tells us that everyone has to return to the same place they started from. Life is an endless journey, and if we look back every time, we can't reach the destination.' Swami's voice echoed in his ears.

The surface was tumultuous with moonlight, and the beauty of the sea seemed to be calling him to explore its depths.

He sat on a big stone and dipped his legs down to touch the waves. He threw pebbles in the water. Suddenly he felt something. There were ripples in the water. He tried to see the source, but that was beyond his view. He grew anxious to find the source, and after watching the water for a long time he noticed some movement. A dark figure was in the water. Aryan was flummoxed when he saw the figure was in a boat.

He was quiet but different thoughts were racing through his mind. The boat approached.

'Yes, just like fish, man can also swim through the tides of the sea, from one place to the other...' Swami's teaching was quite fresh in his memory, and he was trying to correlate the same with the situation he was observing.

From a distance, he recognised the dark figure's as being none other than a girl. She brought her vessel onto the muddy shore, a few meters from Aryan. Aryan couldn't help but stare at her as she got out of the boat. As she was trying to walk away from the boat, she got stuck in the mud, and lost one of her anklets, struggling in the mud.

'Chham chham.' The sound of the anklets disturbed Aryan's concentration. He ran towards the sound and saw the girl was in trouble. As soon as Aryan rescued her trapped legs, the girl ran away from the site towards the forest.

She had been scared, seeing Aryan bare from head to toe. To avoid him, she ran into the woods. Aryan picked up the anklet and was drawn back to memories of the 'chham chham' sound. Aryan was confused and at the same time, he was attracted to the sound. He followed her into the forest. They chased each other for some times and finally Ritwi stopped. Aryan whispered something into her ears that made her understand he wasn't there to harm her. The only thing then bothered Ritwi was Aryan's nakedness.

'This forest is not a safe place for you, girl… Trust me; I won't harm you. I am here to explore the deep sea beyond.' Aryan tried to convince her to come back with him to the boat.

'I am here to explore the world too. This means we are a part of the same journey!' Ritwi whispered.

They went back to the boat, and climbed in.

19. Journey Commences to Unfold the Mystery

Ritwi could feel the softness of Aryan's hand, as he tied the anklet to her left ankle. Bemused, Ritwi kept on looking with her head bent sideways, just like a rosy headed crane. Aryan bent down, holding Ritwi's foot on one of his knees. He was lost in his own imagination.

After a sudden jerk, the boat became still, and it stopped sailing forward. Without any obstruction in sight, they became suspicious of some danger. Aryan jumped in the water, while Ritwi monitored his motions.

A sudden squeal distracted Ritwi and made her turn back in its direction. A girl struggling to keep her head above water was crying aloud. She was looking at Ritwi, babbling something incomprehensible, irritation and agony visible on her face.

She had golden hair, which shone in the moonlight. Her hair seemed

127

dry despite her being in the water. With a slight stroke, the girl moved towards the boat. The up thrust revealed the upper half of the girl's bare body. By then, Aryan had hopped onto the boat.

The half-naked girl squealed again. She seemed to be signaling to them not to move forward. Ritwi, unable to understand the language, started shouting. Aryan put his hand on Ritwi's shoulder, pacifying her, and replied to the girl in the same unfamiliar language, leaving Ritwi stunned.

Ritwi bombarded him with questions.

'Wait! Don't just throw me off-guard…' Aryan managed to reply.

Ritwi stared at him and the unknown girl, half submerged in water, watching as they interacted in an incomprehensible language. She tried to put pieces of this scene together to make some sense of it.

'A beautiful girl with golden hair, in a dark, lonely place, deep inside the water. How is it possible to stay so long in the water without any movement of hands or legs?'

Aryan turned to Ritwi after concluding his chat.

'The girl is Sunheri. She is asking us not to move forward and instead return to where we came from. An invisible protective layer that we can't break or penetrate has obstructed our path. To go forward, we need permission.'

'Who is she? Does she possess some magical powers? How can she dare to obstruct us? What is she doing here alone?' asked Ritwi.

'She is a mermaid, Matsya-Kanya, half fish and half human.'

Sunheri jumped up from the water, and what Ritwi saw left her dumbstruck. She had heard stories about the Matsya-Kanyas in her childhood. 'They actually exist?' was all she could manage to say.

The Matsya-Kanya looked exactly as she had imagined from the stories. She was a human above the waist, but below the waist, she was a fish with scales and fins.

'Why is she asking us to go back? Why can't we move forward?' Ritwi asked.

'According to beliefs of their clan, humans are unfaithful, selfish and morally degraded. They believe we are the most impure of souls. The human achieves or tries to achieve things by hook or by crook, no matter whether it hurts the system or Mother Nature.'

By that time, many Matsya-Kanyas had appeared around the boat, jumping hither and thither. Seeing so many of them, Ritwi was mesmerised. Aryan was trying to convince the Matsya-Kanya, Sunheri, to let them pass. He tried to explain that both of them had no evil intentions towards her people, they were just on a trip to enjoy the ocean in the moonlight.

A Matsya-Kanya emerged from the deep water, a glittering crown on her head. As she appeared above the surface with a wand in her hand, all the other Matsya-Kanyas positioned themselves and welcomed her with bowed heads.

'I wonder if she is the leader or queen of the clan?' Ritwi whispered.

'So it seems,' Aryan replied.

The crowned Matsya-Kanyawas seated in an open shell pulled by sea horses. She came closer to the boat. Sunheri described the situation to the crowned Matsya-Kanya. After listening, the crowned Matsya-Kanya raised her eyes towards Aryan and Ritwi. Seeing her sweet eyes, Ritwi moved back, hiding behind Aryan, though she kept peeping from there.

'WHY ARE YOU HERE? WHO ARE YOU?' asked the crowned Matsya-Kanya, at an unbearably loud volume, so loud that Ritwi had to raise her hands to cover her ears.

'We have no intention of harming any of you for any reason,' Aryan replied .

The sound of her own language calmed the queen. 'What do you want, boy? You are no ordinary human, I see. What provoked you to enter our world?'

'For years, we have been living under rules and restrictions, due to which we had to stay within boundaries. For the first time we have crossed our boundaries, and we are eager to explore the vast world in a limited time. We have no other intention. We were unaware of your boundaries.'

'How do you know our language, who are you and where are you from?'

'I'm Aryan, Swami Brahmanand's pupil. He taught me every language spoken on land, water and air; he passed the knowledge on to me, and gave me the power to interact with living beings so that I could help them in some way. I don't know where I am from. I have been residing in the dark forest for long years with my mother. She was the first human I saw. For the first time, I am delighted to be out of my restricted world, exploring more.'

'You seem honest to me. I might allow you to enter in my world of mermaids, but with a condition!'

Ritwi came forward a bit anxiously. Aryan was prepared to hear the condition. He waited. The crowned mermaid asked Aryan whether he was prepared or not. In acceptance, he nodded his head slowly. The crowned mermaid moved her eyes towards Ritwi and desired to know her stand. Ritwi had a questioning face. After Aryan explained the situation and the question, Ritwi nodded her head vigorously. The crowned mermaid smiled, and her subjects did the same.

The crowned mermaid lifted her left hand, closed her eyes and moved the wand over the open palm. A shining silver vessel appeared. It seemed a liquid diamond was gazing at them in the moonlight. She passed the pot to Sunheri and instructed her to give it to Aryan and Ritwi.

'This is my condition and your test. This is Charan-Amrit of Lord Vishnu's Matsya-Avatar. You will have to consume this, for your souls to be purified. Only then will you be allowed in our territories.'

Aryan took the pot from Sunheri's hand. He lifted it to consume half of it and then passed it on to Ritwi. After drinking the Charan-Amrit, Ritwi felt choked. She coughed and sneezed continuously. Aryan tried to help her but was unable to. After some time, Ritwi appeared calm. When she raised her face, her eyes were filled with tears. She closed her eyes, and the tears rolled down. She seemed to have lost her burdens, become free and relaxed. She wiped her eyes, which sparkled with purity.

Now it was Aryan's turn. He experienced sudden pain in his whole body, which was unbearable. He moaned with pain and kneeled down. A sparkling filled the entire boat. Ritwi closed her eyes as she couldn't bear the sight. After a few moments, she opened her eyes and was amazed to see that Aryan had transformed. His physique was no longer that of a boy, but a man. His chest had become shapely, broader, his abdomen displayed muscles developed with hard labour, his wrist and biceps had grown to give him a warrior's look and his back slimmed to a 'V'. He was beardless as well. Bewildered, Aryan looked at the mermaids and asked, 'How?'

The crowned mermaid just smiled and said, 'Welcome to our world

Aryan. We are happy to extend this invitation to your partner.'

The other mermaids chuckled among themselves rushed towards the boat. They pushed the boat ahead. Now there was no obstruction; the boat passed ahead.

'Aryan, I've never seen pure soul like yours. I'm impressed by your guts and your talent. The physical changes that you see are due to the Charan-Amrit. It purifies a human's soul, and if the soul is pure, it transforms the physical structure and makes him robust and healthy. It improves all the essential qualities of a human. I had never found such a human; you are the first I have seen to have received this boon,' the mermaid said. Aryan thanked her for everything. He was about to translate the interaction to Ritwi, but she placed her fingers over his lips and stopped him.

'Now I understand everything, the language, this new world and all other things,' Ritwi replied to the questions visible in Aryan's eyes.

'Girl, this is because you have entered into our world after consuming the Charan-Amrit. As long as you are in our world, you can interact with us without any trouble. Once you leave our territory, you will lose this power, but your soul will remain purified for a long time. Enjoy your travels here!' The crowned mermaid said.

Aryan bent and felt the water with his palm. Living shells, starfish and many other aquatic animals were passing the boat and Aryan and Ritwi were mesmerised by the sight. Ritwi waved to the mermaids all around, and they returned the favour, unaware of the meaning of the signal. The sea horses were moving on the surface of the water, and the mermaids were diving up and down.

'Here ends our territory. Aryan, this is a gift from us, accept it.'

The queen handed him a white conch and said, 'If you are in trouble in the sea, or nearby on the shore, just blow air into the shell, and we will be there for you. Good luck to both of you on your journey, and take care. We will meet sooner or later, but you will be remembered as a special guest forever. Luck be with you.'

As the boat passed their territory, Aryan turned back to bid goodbye. Ritwi was behind him, and after some time, she placed her hand on his shoulder. Aryan turned back, his eyes fixed on Ritwi. Eyes closed, she leant forward and placed her lips on his. This sensation was entirely new for Aryan. As the sensation aroused him, he closed his eyes and wrapped his hands around Ritwi. He placed one of his hands on her waist and the other on her shoulder and pulled her closer.

A whirring in the air and sensation of something tying up their bodies distracted them. They tried to move but failed. Aryan with his strong body sought to free himself and after a lot of struggle, he was able to loosen the wrappings. Aryan angled his head and looked around. He found their boat stuck on an island and some dark figures rolling on the land. Aryan struggled again and loosened the grip a bit more. The rolling creatures were approaching the boat. It was dark, and Ritwi was unable to see anything, but Aryan could. When they reached the boat, the creatures stopped and stood up straight.

He saw something entirely new. The creatures were small, with bald heads, hairy bodies, burning hot eyes with no eyelids, little hands. He was facing dwarfs. They had moved by rolling themselves in balls, not running or walking.

A few of them boarded the dinghy, and the others stood nearby, alert. The dwarfs who had boarded the boat pushed Aryan and Ritwi from the boat. They landed on the dwarfs waiting outside, and soon a long line formed. Aryan and Ritwi slid over the rolling dwarfs. The movement was extremely smooth barring the tickling feel. Ritwi and Aryan were taken into a cave.

The dwarfs placed them on the floor inside. Aryan and Ritwi struggled to untie themselves.

'Aryan, can you use your power to break this thing?'

'I am unable to; it is quite strong, even for me.'

20. The Land of Dwarfs

A dim light tore the darkness, forcing Ritwi and Aryan to look towards the entrance of the underground cave. A dwarf holding a light-source object entered the cave, followed by the howling and beating of drums. The tiny fingers on the leather wrapped drum worked magnificently. Another dwarf blew into a flute-like instrument, his fingers worked on the holes in the body of the pipe. A huge group of dwarfs, covered in bark, started dancing to the beat and tune of the musical instruments. The female dwarfs came in after the males. They were carrying jugs, eatables, chickens and cups. Then, at last, the children followed. Their strange language, actions, behaviour seemed intriguing. Their chest and abdomen were evenly covered in hair, and their backs were decorated with dark green dye.

All the dwarfs assembled inside the cave in disciplined order, the men and women sitting in pairs and the toddlers standing behind the elders.

All the cups and other items were placed in the centre under the supervision of an old dwarf carrying a stick, who appeared to be the head of the group. On his command, all heads bent down in prayer.

Stones and bones were distributed, and burning logs were placed in different corners of the wide cave. The couples were dancing holding chickens. They killed the chickens by biting their necks.

The sight made Aryan and Ritwi sick.

'Even though Chandaliyan used to kill animals and birds for training and food, I have never seen such fury. They are not normal. How can they be so cruel?' Ritwi whispered to herself.

'Beyond the sea, life is uncertain and different; I have heard that. But seeing this, the culture of playing with blood and with someone's life, the unimaginable brutality, it puts a question mark on humanity. Are they humans or some other species?' Aryan was confused. He tried moving, but the strong rope, made up of animal skins, did not allow him to.

They could only stare helplessly and grin at the group. The dwarfs poured alcohol in their small glasses and enjoyed consuming it while dancing. Ritwi was dying of thirst and hunger. She was unable to bear it and started coughing and making sounds to draw their attention. One girl watched Ritwi curiously. Ritwi turned her face away from the raw food offered by the child, showing no interest, and Aryan did the same. Then the toddler offered the wine jug. Ritwi, despite being exhausted and hardly able to move, somehow gulped it down, only spilling some of it on the ground. Aryan watched, until a new sound drew their attention.

Those dwarfs hugged each other and smelled their bodies, crawling over each other and tasting them with their small black tongues. Ritwi was able to sense by their movements and expressions that all of them were making love. But Aryan was merely looking at the dwarfs; it was quite a new experience for him because previously he had only seen animals making love in the forest. Just like their savage feasting, this was an open intercourse with no sense of intimacy. Ritwi looked at Aryan and then immediately looked away when her eyes met his. Aryan felt that Ritwi too was behaving in a different manner, but he was not aware of her emotions and feelings, which left him confused and curious.

'What are you trying to figure out? How can you stare without any hesitation? This is not normal, and yet you are so calm,' Ritwi said.

'It seems you want to ask something…' Aryan said.

'Hmm… I am not feeling well in this place,' she said, looking awkwardly at the dwarfs.

'What is the problem? This is natural, and they are merely expressing their love,' he said.

'But your face says something else; you are constantly staring at them.'

'Yes… I am trying to understand the culture, and it's new for me even though I have seen something like this earlier in the forest,' Aryan replied.

'Are you attracted by it?'

'Expressing love for the opposite sex is the precursor to the reproduction mechanism in nature, but in the forest, I have seen animals getting involved in a manner entirely different from these people.' Aryan was quite open about his questions and thoughts. But Ritwi was bemused by his innocence.

'I have never met anyone like this. Maybe the gods sent him for me,' Ritwi thought.

The rites of the dwarfs had begun with drinks and dance and ended with intimacy. They fell over each other and slept there on the ground. All lights went off, except one in the corner. Ritwi was unable to see now, thanks to the low light. All she could hear was snoring, which was increasing gradually in volume. She was not aware, but it was the effect of the wine that she consumed. Intoxicated, Ritwi felt the warm breaths of Aryan on her neck. She felt as if Crystal were near her, instead of Aryan. Closing her eyes, she could imagine Crystal lowering his face down towards hers to plant a kiss on her quivering lips, but as soon as she felt the hot breaths of Crystal on her face so close she moved her face aside, and opened her eyes.

'Why? I love you, and you love me, then why this shyness? It is a symbol of our love.'

'Crystal, I haven't yet decided on you. I love the way you love me, and the way you expressed it on the canvases,' Ritwi whispered. Meanwhile, Aryan was mesmerised to see Ritwi lost so deeply in her dreams.

'Come out of your dreams…' Aryan whispered in her ears.

Slowly she opened her eyes and smiled. 'Sorry, was I murmuring something absurd to you?'

'No… but you were talking about love and some canvases…' Aryan said.

'I am not feeling well. I feel nauseous.'

'Take a deep breath and hold it, close your eyes and forget this nausea. The thought in your mind will awaken your sensual abilities and impede vomiting,' Aryan whispered in her ears while her eyes were closed.

While whispering, Ritwi felt Aryan's hot breath on her shoulder, and she felt good. Her body was cold and shivering as she had nothing in her tummy and the whole day had been spent on the water. On top of that, she had consumed the unfamiliar wine. As soon as Ritwi felt comfortable she rested her chin on Aryan's shoulder, and she started speaking with her quivering lips.

'Please come closer, it makes me feel good. I'm feeling cold, so please hold me tight. I need warmth,' Ritwi insisted.

'Our body temperature drops when we are tired. Eventually, we feel cold, and our body starts shivering. In an emergency, a human can transfer his or her warmth to another person, just by coming in contact with that person physically,' Aryan recalled some of the teachings of Swamiji.

21. Amalgamating the Souls

Aryan was thankful that his well-built body was quite resistant to moderate temperature variations. He embraced Ritwi warmly so that she could feel better.

The silk cloth wrapped around her breasts was loosened by this contact, unintentionally exposing her cleavage. Aryan's nose rubbed against her forehead. Her breasts brushed his broad chest. The embrace aroused Ritwi. She couldn't stop her lips from resting on his. Aryan was still gazing at her, a question in his eyes. He knew this kiss was wilder than the preceding one on the boat. She tasted dusty and salty as he was sweating.

Bewilderment was clearly visible on Aryan's face, as he was trying to figure out what was going on. She held him close. Her face was tilted to his, her eyelids heavy. She allowed her body to tremble, unchecked. Aryan submitted to the passionate kiss. They could feel their hearts pounding, and the sounds of their breathing became harsh and noisy.

'I can hear the voice of your heart. Is this the time we have longed for...?' Ritwi mumbled in Aryan's ear.

'My soul longs for oceans of love, it longs for sands of devotion and purity and for those realms of time where our story was written years ago,' Aryan murmured. His innocence roused Ritwi further.

'How can he talk about love?' Ritwi wondered. Aryan seemed so different, unaware of the language of love, but she still expected him to make love to her.

She didn't bother questioning him, afraid of making him stop abruptly. She just wanted to feel the heat, to feel him tight. The touch of his skin was quite sensational to her. Aryan was experiencing the stronger side of desire for the first time, and each act of his gave Ritwi immense pleasure. She had never experienced such intimacy before, but she played teacher to this innocent pupil of love.

'Something is separating our skin, my girl. I am dying to explore the immense beauty of the sea... I am dying to explore...' the harsh sounds of his breathing completed the incomplete sentence.

This time, Ritwi felt as if someone else were speaking in her ears, not Aryan. But when she tried to figure out who, she failed to do so. Aryan himself was responding now, and she was swept off on a wave of desire.

She had never dreamt of sleeping with such a strange man, and reality proved wilder than any dream. She felt the necessity of undressing herself, maybe she desired to shed her body and offer it to Aryan, the man of her dreams. She let her bare skin hug his bare skin. She kissed his neck and moved her fingers over his eyes, trying to see the beauty of her love within. All she could see was his innocence and some rapidly disappearing questions. Then she closed her eyes for a moment, maybe to see if her conscience was in tandem with her physical desire.

Abruptly, she opened her eyes, looked into his. She felt shy and turned her back to him. Now Aryan was behind her. Aryan tried to understand her sudden withdrawal.

'You are the man of my dreams, but I don't know why I am failing to convey my desires through love…' Ritwi said.

Aryan wrapped his arm around her waist, pulling her close to his body. He started kissing her shoulders, neck, chin and her hair. Slowly, he explored her face with his hands. The softness of his fingers and his warm breath roused sensations in her, and she was losing control. She turned again towards Aryan and looked into his eyes. She saw Aryan's eyes moving, exploring her beauty. Aryan was amazed by her beauty. It was not the first time he was seeing a woman in her nakedness, but this was different for him. He felt different, he felt like smelling her, tasting her and he started circling his finger around her navel.

'You smell wonderful, and your beauty is killing me… You may call me desperate, but I am not…'

When she heard this, in surprise she moved her eyes towards Aryan. She found his bright eyes were ablaze with excitement.

'I want you to burn for me…like the rising of the sun is essential to life, the merging of you with me is the core time.' Ritwi felt the urge to play now, distancing her body from Aryan. Her body was shaking, and she felt Aryan's hand over her arm, reaching out for her.

Aryan pulled her towards him. He placed his hand gently on her body. Aryan moved his legs between hers. Ritwi separated her bare legs, allowing his left leg to drape over her left leg. He rubbed his legs over hers gently. She took his hand and placed it between her legs. She put her hand over his hand that was caressing her breasts. The rhythm of their heartbeats was synchronised, and he grasped her neck and moved his lips over her body very softly. The heat of her body was increasing, and so was Aryan's. She felt hypersensitive and in no time, she spread her legs wide, hungry to make intense love.

She felt the hard shaft rubbing warmly against her thigh. Aryan felt a current flowing through his body, and he felt strange when he leaked pre-cum over her bare thighs. She felt the warmth once again, and the sensation of the creamy fluid drove her wild. She lowered her hand to touch his hard body, and she felt like brushing his penis over her clitoris.

Aryan penetrated her. Ritwi loved the way he felt inside her. She felt the warm body inside her, and she felt it growing harder and making its existence felt. He moved back gently, trying to make her feel at ease. She felt something tearing apart inside her.

'I fear I may hurt you... again!' Aryan's voice was all that she could hear.

The words woke her and suddenly made her feel as though she were sleeping with a stranger, but it was hard for her to maintain her distance from him now.

With each thrust inside her, she felt like dying. She was unable to bear the pain.

Her eyes were closed. She suffered sweet pain and bled as well.

Chandaliyan was viewing Ritwi and Aryan's intimacy in a blood-filled vessel. He crept trying to see the boy's face; it was obscured by the blaze imparted by the Amrit. Ritwi's face was clearly visible with sweat droplets running down her forehead. Chandaliyan seemed to be worried, and irritation was visible on his face.

He paced to and fro in the room, and seeing Chandaliyan's tension and irritation, he asked, 'What's the matter, where is my daughter, is she alright?'

Chandaliyan stood up, and the blood-filled vessel's image disappeared.

'Nothing to be worried about, Chief. She will be back soon, have patience.'

Scenes of intimacy were revolving in his head, and he was unable to believe what he had seen moments earlier. Chandaliyan was aware that things could hardly disturb the love birds; he was unable to control what was happening on the island of the dwarfs. In short, there was nothing he could do.

It was midnight, and Ritwi felt that things had changed for her.

'You want me to torment you more...?' she heard someone saying, but this time, she wasn't disturbed. Before she could think, she found herself speaking.

'Yes... till my body weep with the tears of lust.' Her voice was shaking, and her breath was high and rapid.

Intense passion took over, and two bodies disappeared into one. Ritwi felt something different when Aryan's cum was released inside her. Aryan too felt it, but he was unaware of the happenings.

Their movements were as fast as the waves crashing on the shore, as moist as mud soaking in rain.

'It's beyond everything; I sacrificed my soul and this moment I want you more and more...' Aryan murmured into her ears.

Aryan came out of her and kissed her, his body's sweat mixed with that of Ritwi. She moved her face towards Aryan, stared at his face.

Exhaustion was visible on his face. He allowed his body to fall on the floor, and he breathed long and hard. His eyes were moist. Ritwi behaved differently now; she was not able to face him. She lowered her eyelids and looked here and there. Then she tried to look in his eyes, tried to sense his emotions but she felt confused.

'Are you alright?'

She nodded her head gently in response.

'I was unsure whether my body could bear it. But it was wonderful,' she said, looking down.

'I have never done this with any man, and I don't know how it all happened,' she continued.

'What happened? Do you regret it?' Aryan asked.

'No... I was confused before making love with you, but now I feel good. I want to respect the man in you. I feel as though I have known you for quite a long time. Maybe the journey of our hearts began years ago, and we were destined to comfort each other like this.'

'Destiny and time may flirt with each other, but I won't let them decide my fate. It took years to feel you, my love.'

145

Perhaps this was the timeless journey of two souls. Though relative strangers, after tasting love they felt as though they had known each other for ages. They felt the magic of their hearts and wanted more and more, desiring to explore each other's bodies. They felt strange and awkward at times while making love, but something held their love, so close and tight, a bond that could never be weakened, a bond that a soul wants to stay tied to. It was not only desire that made them intimate; perhaps it was that one soul wanted to rest on its mate. Possibly the soul had found the home of its love, the destination which it had desired to reach, walking side by side. The two closed their eyes, her head resting on his broad chest. She felt heavenly comfort in his arms covering her body, his chin touching her long brown hair. The difference between a dreamy reality and dreams faded as they slept cozily nestled against each other.

After a while, they felt choked, and started murmuring very softly, maybe they were in their dreams. A blurred image of an old temple and silhouette of two persons approaching each other was partially visible. Before the two could meet each other, they heard an unusual noise of bells clinking. The noise was no less than the sounds of temple bells at dawn. But strangely, it was actually midnight. The sound grew louder with time, and someone's cry of pain was mixed with it. Their eyes opened, surprised, staring at each other. The vibrations and the sound faded, and they assumed it had all been a dream.

22. Encountering the Deformed Beast!

A furry hand with long fingers and pointed nails motioned noiselessly, seeking to grab the little dwarf girl who was fast asleep. The baby dwarf started squealing as soon as the wild hand, which resembled a deformed human hand, found its grip.

Aryan and Ritwi, who had just opened their eyes from the nightmare, were distracted instantly by the squeal. Ritwi saw the little girl who had served her alcohol squealing in pain. She looked for a means to rescue her.

With the loud screech, two of the dwarfs woke from their sleep, but they did nothing but watch as the girl was hauled away.

The whole incident left everyone dumbstruck. Finally having managed to loosen the ropes, Aryan raced out of the entrance, seeking to find the child.

As soon as they came back to their senses, one of the dwarfs noticed that Aryan was missing and alerted the others. One after the other, all the dwarfs came back to their senses. With time, more of them got up from slumber, unaware of the incident. The two dwarfs discussed something in their language and after hearing the story, the other dwarfs became struck with fear. Since no one could find Aryan, they instantly rolled towards Ritwi, who was sitting idle, totally confused and terrified.

The dwarfs were crying aloud, especially the two who had watched the little one be snatched away. Ritwi figured out that they were related to the child. She could see agony in their eyes. They picked up the loosened rope and tied it around her again, this time so tightly that she screamed in pain.

'Please leave me…please!' Seeing that no one was willing to listen to her, she continued glancing towards the entrance with fading requests and sobs.

Far from the cave, Aryan was standing lonely on the sands, completely drenched in sweat and sand. He was puffing vigorously and still vigilant for any sign of a possible threat. Suddenly, he marked some traces on the sand, and followed them anxiously. But after a few steps, he did not find anything to follow and when he was about to turn back, he was distracted by a feeble sound, a little ahead. The sound was coming from a bush, and there he marked some movement on the sand. Aryan moved towards the bush attentively.

With a sudden jerk, he fell down as some unknown figure overcame him, and he lost balance. He turned his face towards the movement of the unknown figure; he found a beast growling with saliva dropping down from its mouth. Its red eyes were burning with fire, and his forelegs were bunched, ready to pounce. It was of a kind he had never seen before. Built like a big wild ape, the beast had a horrific appearance. With a great roar, the beast jumped forward to attack Aryan.

Terrorised yet steady, Aryan closed his eyes for a moment and recalled the teachings of Swamiji.

'When unarmed, you need not fear. Your fear will make you lose your battle, and with a strong-will you can bag victory…' Swamiji's words echoed in his mind.

Even though he had never faced such a situation, Aryan clenched his fingers in a fist within the moment. He was ready to meet the strange wild beast and fight back.

The beast began to move ferociously, but Aryan was prepared to dodge it. Every attack from the beast was either resisted or avoided by Aryan and his fists acted upon the beast with glory. Thanks to his consumption of the magical Charan-Amrit, his punches were very powerful, surprising Aryan himself. The beast was unable to harm Aryan in any possible way. It was jumping above Aryan to confuse him but thanks to hard punches from Aryan to its chest, it was in pain, weakened and exhausted. With a strong punch to its head, it fell with its face hitting the sand, and lay there without any movement.

Aryan went closer to study it, and suddenly the long nails of its hand moved up and scratched his face. The beast stood up. It started scratching Aryan's back with its long nails.

'Never grow overconfident while you are in combat,' he seemed to hear Swamiji say.

Aryan, realising his mistake, yelled to regain willpower and strength. He moved his hands back, and with his elbow, hit the beast's jaw, pushing it away. The beast's mouth started bleeding with the blow, and it yelled in pain. Aryan moved close again, but another blow on his back made him collapse. He flinched away, avoiding another blow, this one from a second beast. The second beast dodged Aryan and went instead to the first.

'Are you alright?'

Aryan was shocked to hear a human voice from the beast. It was caressing its injured partner exactly as a human does.

'Who are you?' Aryan asked the beast. The second beast, moved its red eyes towards Aryan. It seemed helpless and angry at the same time.

Aryan was confused, but his attention was drawn by the little dwarf, who was hidden in the bush. She seemed struck with terror and was physically injured, Aryan caught hold of her hand in a protective way, but his eyes were fixed on the strange beasts.

'We are cursed. Don't cross us, I warn you. Leave the dwarf and go on your way. Don't mess with us, or you will lose everything,' the beast growled.

'Who are you? You speak as a human and have a somewhat similar build,' said Aryan.

'We feed on these dwarfs. We are under a spell to feed on them. Leave us alone,' the beast said.

The baby dwarf was holding Aryan tight around his legs. Saliva was coming out of the beast's mouth.

Carrying the baby dwarf, Aryan moved towards the crying beast. As Aryan was moving ahead, the growling was rising higher.

'I'm not here to harm you. You can trust me to be a friend. You say you are bewitched. If so, there must be a way to release you from this curse!'

Both beasts looked at each other, confused. They were still suspicious of him.

'How can we share our secrets with him? How can we tell him about the land?' one beast was whispering to the other.

Aryan broke the silence, understanding the doubts of the beasts. He tried to convince them as much as he could.

'I am expecting you to share with me your defining curse… You can trust me…'

The child started crying. Aryan felt the urge to take the child back to her parents. But at the same time, he wanted to understand the beasts, and why they needed to feed on the dwarfs.

'Trust me; I can help you, but only if you share the secrets of your life with me. You need not feed on these dwarfs. Where is the land you are talking about?'

The beast told him everything, and at the end it pointed its long fingers, showing the land. For the blowing winds and the dust, it was not visible.

'Promise me you will keep your word,' Aryan said.

The beast closed its eyes in acceptance. After getting this assurance, Aryan moved towards the den carrying the little dwarf in his arms.

Unusual sounds were echoing and getting louder when Aryan stepped inside the cave. Ritwi was tied up and was being readied for slaughter by the dwarfs when Aryan entered with the baby dwarf. The baby dwarf started crying, making a loud sound at seeing her parents and community.

With the sound of the baby dwarf, the attention was drawn towards Aryan. Seeing the baby dwarf in Aryan's arms, the dwarfs got excited and rolled towards him. The baby dwarf on seeing her parents approaching jumped from his arms.

The leader and father of the baby dwarf asked the baby how she had managed to escape from the beast and the baby dwarf gave a detailed account. As soon as the dwarf had concluded her tale, the leader instructed his people to release Ritwi.

Ritwi rushed towards Aryan as soon as she was untied. The dwarfs prostrated themselves before Aryan, showing their gratitude to him as he had saved the life of one of their own.

Aryan and Ritwi understood this through their actions and expressions, but were not able to comprehend their language. Aryan was confused about how to interact with them, but then the leader came forward and bowed down to thank him.

'We are obliged to you; you have saved my baby's life when we were about to harm you.'

'Damn, you know our language! How? Do all of you know this language?' Aryan asked.

'No, only I know the language. I'm the leader and with my experience of long years, I have gotten acquainted with several languages.'

'Aryan, let's leave this place. I don't feel comfortable here,' Ritwi whispered.

'No lady, please don't get annoyed, do not misunderstand us. We tied you up under the impression that you had some connection to the beasts.'

'Leave those doubts behind. From now on, they will never harm you, I promise that,' Aryan said to the leader.

'We would really like to be freed now,' Ritwi said.

'I've a request. Please spend a day with us so that we can express our gratitude. Please...'

'No Aryan, do not accept. I sense something fishy,' Ritwi whispered to him.

Aryan looked into Ritwi's horrified eyes and then at the dwarf leader.

'Accepted...' Aryan said.

Ritwi was shocked by this response, but Aryan consoled her.

The celebration started in an exciting manner. It was the first time any of the dwarfs had been saved from the jaws of the beast, and hence it was a moment of celebration for everyone. The dwarfs treated Aryan and Ritwi as saintly people who had come in disguise to their clan to rescue them from the deadly beasts. After the day of celebration in which the dwarfs paid their respects with a royal touch to Aryan for saving their girl's life, they were tired, and went to bed exhausted.

At midnight when everyone was deeply asleep, Aryan got up and so did Ritwi. They were prepared to leave the place without the knowledge of dwarfs. But with their movements and sounds, the leader got up from his deep sleep. He rolled near Aryan and Ritwi and asked about their departure. Aryan informed him that it was the right time to begin his journey as he couldn't bear sunlight and he had to move a long way ahead. The leader ordered all of the dwarfs to get up as their saintly guests were leaving. They got up, and everyone rolled towards the shore near the boat. They loaded the boat with all the things required for a journey. And, as the boat was ready to sail off, Aryan and Ritwi thanked the clan for everything. The boat sailed off towards the dark horizon. The baby dwarf whom Aryan had saved was in tears, looking towards the disappearing boat and her saviour.

23. The Mysterious Land!

The boat was about to reach a new shore when a fog rolled in. They were dashed onto a rock.

'The destination has arrived,' Aryan said.

'But how will we find it? Did the beast give you information with which to identify it?'

'Yes, but for now we should move into the forest. The sun has started showing its gleam and in no time it will show its face. We must get inside the forest, as the beast had described. The sun rays will not be able to penetrate its darkness.'

'But I'm afraid. This forest is pitch dark! At least wait for the sun to rise.'

'Don't worry; I'm with you.'

'But the darkness…and this land seems to be terrifying.'

'Yes it is. That's why it is called the mysterious land, where you can find your real existence.'

155

'I don't think it would be wise for us to go on. Let's move back or wait until the sunrise, please Aryan...'

'Both the requests you made I will be unable to keep. I'm under an oath. Neither can I go back without completing this work, nor can I wait until sunrise.'

Aryan caught hold of Ritwi's hand and climbed the rock. Before the sun rays tore apart the fog, they were on the edge of the forest.

'Why are you so scared of the sunlight? You are brave and powerful enough to face all sort of troubles in the dark, then why not in the daylight?'

Ritwi stopped Aryan by pulling his hands.

'Wait, Aryan, I believe in you, but I'm not yet convinced of your reasons.'

Aryan was speechless and by then the sun rays shone on his face. He squealed in pain. Ritwi was stunned to see it. Aryan closed his eyes and rushed ahead towards the forest.

Ritwi was astounded to see the burn on Aryan's back.

'How did this happen!'

'Promises are not made to be broken. Also, curses are awoken when we seek to push beyond the law.'

'You mean you are living a cursed life?' Ritwi asked.

'Not exactly, but my skin supports the twilight, not the sun. Sometimes I feel this to be a curse, but this is the darkest truth I have been told right from childhood. I tried to disobey the law; the consequence is in front of you.'

'I'm extremely sorry, Aryan. You had to pay for my stubborn questioning.'

'Don't feel guilty. Come, let's go find what we must, and then submerge it in the sea.'

'Aryan, you haven't yet explained to me the story of the beasts.'

Aryan was walking briskly in the dark, dense forest. Ritwi stopped protesting and forcing Aryan for the details of the conversation with the beast. But finally, submitting to this loving and childishly stubborn girl, he spilt it out, using the words of the beast.

'A few years ago, my brother and I lived in a village far from here. We were very wealthy. After our father's death, we got involved in many antisocial activities, and thus came under the influence of our land's chief. He was a lecher. Though we drank, used marijuana and other such things to stay high all the time, we respected women and the poor. The chief was a real moron; he always provoked us, but we ignored it.

'Once, a Brahmin couple had to face a bit of nuisance from the chief, for which we both had to pay. The couple had arrived to organize some spiritual work as part of the annual celebration of our village. The chief attended the ceremony, but he was weaving some plan which no one was aware of. After the completion of the ceremony, the couple had to move to the palace where we both were resting. After making us high, the chief threw us completely out of our senses. As soon as the couple arrived in the room, we misbehaved with them, especially the woman. They were very spiritual, religious and pure but because of our misbehaviour, they were hurt and put both of us under a spell, giving us this beast form as we had behaved like beasts.

'The next day, when we regained our senses and recalled the incident, we were really ashamed of our deeds, and we approached the couple to beg their pardon. At first, they didn't believe us, but later they were convinced that we felt guilty. They consoled us; their curse was going to come true but out of sympathy the woman said, maybe God can help.

'Before we began our journey, we consulted with the saint of the land, Chandaliyan, and he instructed us to move to a mysterious land. It was believed that he could see the future and had the capacity to change it. The day we were about to begin our journey we heard the Brahmin couple had been murdered, and the Chief and the saint had spread a rumour that we had killed them in revenge. We were not involved with the heinous act in any way, but the villagers marched to kill us. Anyhow, we managed to escape and entered the place, where Chandaliyan would conduct his prayers. We asked him for the truth and learned that everything had been planned by him. Our feelings for him changed drastically. We were about to reveal the truth to other people, but with the help of black magic, he changed everything. He decided our future. According to him, we were supposed to move to a mysterious land and find a half broken evil statue, hidden in the dense forest, where even in the day the sun rays do not fall on the ground. There is a guard who never allows anyone to enter the area near the statue. We needed to find the evil statue and submerge it in the sea with fire on it. Only then could we be released from the curse. The saint added that it would take years to be freed from this curse. And thanks to this, his secret would remain a secret forever.

'We managed to reach the mysterious land and found many mirages there. The place was a puzzle just like a Chakravyuha. Evil's idol was at the centre of seven phases. In the second stage, we were dying of hunger as we had not carried any food with us. There we found some fresh fruits lying near a tree. With the last bite of the fruit, we turned back, having heard a call filled with rage. It was the guard of the forest; he had accumulated the fruits for his lord, and we had finished all of them. We begged pardon, but he was not in a mood to listen. We tried to make him understand that we were hungry and had hence eaten them. But in anger, he put us under another spell to feed on raw flesh for a lifetime. We were worried about the previous curse already, and this one made us furious, so we attacked the old guard. We lost our human form as soon as we harmed him and turned into beasts. Our human bodies lay on the earth. Here we are feeding on the raw flesh as cursed by the guard and roaming in beast-form as cursed by the brahmin lady. Now with evil's statue, our bones need to be merged in water with fire and only then can we be released from both curses. As this land is avoided by humans, we prefer to reside here, and when hunger overcomes us, we pick one of of the dwafs to feed on.'

Ritwi had noted the mention of Chandilayan, and her suspicions were aroused.

'Did they mention which place they belonged to?'

'No.'

'I know a person named Chandaliyan from our land. Maybe the person they mentioned is not the same one I know, because he is a very kind and godly saint. I know him personally.'

Aryan barely listened as he was moving in the forest as though he were hypnotised. As soon as Ritwi saw his eyes even she was hypnotised, and some unknown and invisible power took over them. Both of them could hear many voices around, but neither of them could see anyone. The voices they could hear were of a couple, and the ringing bell of the temple could be heard. As they listened, they seemed to hear visitors to the temple interacting with the Mahant and his wife.

People were sharing their troubles with the couple, and the couple was guiding them on the rules of life and how to lead their lives. After some time they seemed to see transparent figures appearing before them.

Meanwhile, they had crossed into the second stage of the forest.

Here the transparent figures came to Ritwi and Aryan with folded hands and bent down to touch their feet. They were astonished as they had a feeling of déjà vu.

'This is what the beast said, that we could see our real selves and existence here. But we can't trace any happenings from our previous lives. Did you see any figure and hear its strange voice?' Aryan asked Ritwi.

Ritwi described the forms that she was able to see, and Aryan noted that they shared same visuals. Both of them went in opposite directions, following the mirages around them. The transparent humans led them but finally they turned back. Proceeding towards each other, they met up at a point. Though they were looking at each other, they were thinking 'What is my real existence and identity in this land?'

'We should move ahead. I must find the statue before sunset as you may be afraid of the dark. Let's go,' Aryan said.

Ritwi turned to her right and Aryan to his left. Ritwi looked down, and Aryan looked up.

Then Aryan stopped, shocked by what he saw in front of him. A lady wearing a yellow *saree*, with tilak and vermillion on her forehead, rudraksha beads tied on her arms and neck. She seemed to be a reflection of Aryan in the female form. Ritwi noticed that Aryan had stopped. She herself faced a male, who was standing before her. She was dumbfounded and in fear she caught Aryan's arm.

Both were confused for the moment and extended their hands, as did their alter egos. As their fingertips touched, there was a bright flash of light which filled the dark surroundings and they were forced to close their eyes.

For the moment, everything was still. When they opened their eyes, their replicas had disappeared; they searched for them but couldn't find any trace. Both of them felt they had some relation with the figures; their hearts were pounding because of this unimaginable experience. Not finding any explanation, they proceeded ahead, onto the third stage of the mysterious land.

'See the young lad with the girl, moving here completely naked.'

Aryan could hear this, followed by a chuckle. Soon he could hear several chuckles continuously. He looked around to see anything suspicious.

'Someone is watching us here,' Aryan said.

'Why do you think so?'

'I heard someone talking and chuckling.'

'What did you hear?'

Aryan told her what he had heard and started following the sound of chuckling. But the chuckles were coming from the thick foliage all around them. The trees seemed to reach up to the sky. Aryan craned his neck to look for the source of the noise.

'It seems he is searching for someone; for us,' two voices echoed.

'Don't worry, he can't find us,' a third voice said.

'When you feel your mind is getting distracted and disturbed while trying to focus, then close your eyes. Focus on the imagined white spot in your head and you will be able to settle your fluctuating mind.' Aryan reminded himself of Swamiji's words; he closed his eyes and concentrated.

'What is he doing?' The same voice vibrated in his ear.

Aryan moved his head as his ears caught the direction of the voice. With his eyes closed, he moved towards the voice and bumped against a big tree.

'Oh poor guy, did it hurt you?' These words were followed by numerous chuckles.

24. Questions Unsealed by Nature

Ritwi could hear the whisper, but seeing no one she was alert and frightened at the same time.

'Aryan, what is this sound, where is it coming from?'

Aryan opened his eyes and glanced at the tree.

'Is it you?' he asked the tree.

'What bullshit are you talking Aryan? How can this tree talk!'

'As we humans interact, every living being interacts with itself. They can express their feelings, and the power to communicate with them will allow you to understand their speech.'

'But how do you know the language, how is it audible to you?'

'This is what I'm thinking about…'

Aryan folded his hands and got down on his knees before the tree.

'I know you want to interact with us. Please shower your blessings on us. We will be grateful.'

163

Suddenly the branches of the tree started moving to and fro and the dried leaves fell on the two. Soon all the trees started doing the same, as though happy to share their feelings with someone new.

'So you are the one. We are all happy that after many years, we have found a human who cares and shares with other living beings.'

'What's your name, boy?' a tree asked.

'Aryan, and this is Ritwi.'

'What brings you here to this land...'

'We are here to fulfil a promise, a promise I made to someone.'

'Well, if you are here for the evil statue then turn back the same way you came from...'

'I'm here for the reason you just said and with this, I have to complete a task. But why should I turn back?'

'You are too young to face these circumstances. You may even face death, and this young girl will have to pay for you.'

'Overcoming my fear, I need to achieve success. Death is the only truth of the world and it comes sooner or later, death follows the fear. But it is the end that promises a new life,' Aryan said.

'Boy, you remind me of someone we met scores of years ago. Reveal your identity.'

'I'm the pupil of Swami Brahmanand.'

'Now we have no doubt that you can achieve success. Swami Brahmanand is the person you reminded me of.'

'Had Guruji ever stepped on this land?'

'Yes, he came to this land many years ago. His valuable teachings must have made you wise and powerful enough to face any obstacle, and you will achieve success in every walk of life. But why are you walking completely naked?'

'What does that mean?'

'Being the most knowledgeable human's pupil, you don't know what that means?'

Aryan was silent, and the tree continued.

'Why is your body not covered, boy? There is no trace of any clothing on you.'

'What is clothing?'

'You see the girl? She is covered in clothes. Nature provides you with various things to cover yourself.'

'She is the first human I have met in this condition. From my childhood, I have never seen anyone covering their body with any such thing. I've never felt any awkwardness. Rather, I find my way to be the natural way.'

'But you must cover yourself because you are a grown up now. Your manhood needs to be covered up.'

'What shall I do? Guruji didn't ever say such things to me, and neither did my mother!'

'Cover up your body.'

'But how? I don't have any material, how shall I cover myself up?'

'Come closer to me. My dry bark, can you see it? That shall be your covering. Peel it off me and put it on.'

Aryan peeled the dried bark from the tree and was confused about how to wear it.

'What do you intend to do with this bark?' Ritwi questioned.

'I need to cover my manhood!' Aryan said in a confused voice.

Ritwi stepped close and held the bark in her hands. She bent down with a slight smile on her face. She wrapped the dried bark around Aryan's waist and with the help of thorns, she sewed the pieces together, but it came loose very soon. Instead, she picked up some roots and tied them around his waist to hold the bark.

'Now you look like a young lad.'

'I feel uncomfortable with this bark around me.'

'It is the very first time you have worn it. With time it will be adjusted.'

'I need to know about this land. Why is it considered to be haunted? Why can't humans leave once they come in?'

'Those who are gifted with a pure heart can exit from here, like your Guru did. The only thing is to remember not to tangle with the guard of this forest. The rest you can manage.'

'Where will I find the guard?'

'We haven't seen him for many years. He may be roaming around this land.'

'If he has grown old then there is no need to fear, right?' Aryan asked.

'Don't think that way. Even though he has grown old, he has great powers, and he is gifted. If anyone messes with him, the only thing that remains is ash and bones.'

'I haven't seen any other animal or bird here. What is the reason for that?' Aryan asked.

'No animal can enter this land. If they enter, as I said, they would be burnt to ash.'

'So how do I deal with the guard and where can I find the statue?' Aryan asked.

'Don't mess with the guard. If possible, help him, be polite, avoid any arrogance. You may feel awkward about his lifestyle and appearance, but you must be cordial.

'Next, the statue you are in search of, you will not find it until the guard allows you to do so. It is invisible and is placed at the centre.'

'How will I recognise the place?'

'The patch of land where the statue is hidden is completely barren, not a single blade of grass grows there.'

'Where can I find the bones of the humans?'

'We are not aware of that; the guard can help you.'

'We must leave now. Thank you for your advice.'

They moved towards the centre. Aryan was feeling uneasy because of the bark tied around his waist. Ritwi was enjoying this as he was holding the bark with every step. Their eyes searched for the guard, but he was nowhere to be seen.

25. Past Coincides the Present

Chandaliyan stepped into the guest house of Chief Mathews in Kumbhgarh. Crystal was standing next to the Chief.

'Chief, is this the boy you told me about?'

'Yes. This is Crystal, the brave one.'

Crystal bent in salutation to Chandaliyan.

'Brave boy, come with me. I have something to discuss with you in private. Chief, please hold on for a few moments.'

Crystal followed Chandaliyan for some distance.

'Crystal, do you love Ritwi?'

Crystal was silent as he was a bit confused and felt shy to answer.

'Don't be scared to share this with me. I know everything already. I just want to hear it from you.'

Crystal glanced at Mathews, who was standing at a distance.

Finally, he stated that he loved Ritwi from the depths of his heart, from the very first day they had met.

'So what is your plan for the future? Will you marry her or not?'

'Umm...' Crystal glanced at Mathews.

'I understand your concern. Don't worry, I will manage him. I have decided you are a prospective groom for Ritwi. Let us go to the Chief.'

Both of them moved back towards Chief. As they approached, Chandaliyan said,

'Crystal, today you must go towards your native place and bring your parents here.'

'With your permission, Chief,' Crystal asked with bowed head.

Chandaliyan nodded at Chief to grant permission, and Mathews allowed it and left the place with Chandaliyan.

It was evening, and the sky was reddish and moist. The flags above the palace were flying with pride. Chuckling sounds, along with the sound of the blowing wind, was all that could be heard. A donkey was braying loudly, raising his head towards the palace.

A few children were bullying an insane man. The man had long and dirty hair and ragged clothes, and he was wrapped up in a torn blanket. The children were throwing stones at him, and he was protecting himself by covering himself with the blanket. With every hit, he screamed in pain. Suddenly, hearing hoof beats approaching from a distance, he fell still. Now he didn't yell at the strikes; he was concentrating on the sounds.

169

Crystal was riding a horse, moving next to a horse cart. He was approaching the man and the group of children. The man's eyes followed the moving cart as if he had found something special. His eyes were pinned on the person sitting inside the cart. He picked up some stones. The stones hit the cart explosively. The person seated inside the cart just glanced back and saw the madman gathering the stones. Their eyes showed pity and they sat back.

After gathering some stones in his blanket, the man followed the moving cart, throwing the collected stones at regular intervals.

The cart reached Kumbhgarh Palace's entry where two guards opened the large gate. Most of the stones, thrown madly, missed the cart. And when the cart was entering the yard, beyond the gate, a stone hit the forehead of the bearded person inside the cart. This person reached out and grasped his fellow passenger's hands.

The insane man was satisfied with his hit and started celebrating his victory, raising both of his hands. Even the donkey seemed happy and it started braying again.

Though guards stopped him from entering the palace, even so, the man managed to throw a few more stones which littered the ground.

Seeing the approaching cart near the palace steps, another guard came down to invite its passengers within, followed by the Chief and Chandaliyan. By this time, Crystal had dismounted from his horse and was standing beside his parents.

The bearded person with a hand on his forehead was looking down, and the lady was staring at her husband with worried eyes. Even Crystal was a bit worried looking at his father's swollen forehead.

'Welcome, Crystal!' Chandaliyan said. 'It is an honour to welcome the parents of this brave boy,' he added.

The bearded person warily raised his eyes and instantly lowered them after a quick glance.

Chief was trying to concentrate on the guests but was distracted by Chandaliyan, who asked him to invite the guests inside.

'Crystal… Welcome my boy. I think your parents feel some hesitation, but please feel at ease,' he said.

'He was injured while entering the palace for an insane person hit him with stones. That's why he is looking down, because of pain,' Crystal clarified.

Crystal and his parents climbed the stairs. As they reached Chief and Chandaliyan, Chandaliyan said, 'I think the injury is not very significant, and being the groom's father you mustn't bow your head, it isn't our culture. You must be proud for having brought up a mighty and knowledgeable man like Crystal. Chief, please welcome your future in-laws.'

Chief Mathews stared at Chandaliyan, quite confused. Finally, he stretched his hands forward towards Crystal's father, but didn't get a hand in return. This made Chief feel awkward and a bit irritated. Crystal's father raised his face, but kept his eyes lowered.

Chief was astonished to see a known face behind the beard. He looked at Chandaliyan. Indifferent to the expressions on Chief's face, the priest said, 'Oh, it has swollen badly. You need some first aid. Let's go inside.

'Chief, several times I have told you that you should get rid of that mad man from the road. He is no longer the same Elvin that we knew. Now he is mad; we should not entertain him…'

'I am sorry for your father's condition, Crystal. The man served me a long time ago. Due to an accident, he lost his friend, and now he is losing control of his mind,' Chief explained while walking beside Crystal.

'Crystal, make your parents comfortable in the guest room. I will send some medical aid. Ask them to take rest. We will have a talk with them after a couple of hours. They must be tired from the long journey.'

Chandaliyan and Chief were in a heated discussion. Chief refused to accept what Chandaliyan was trying to make him understand. Finally Chandilayan said:

'Now Chief, it is up to you. What I'm saying is favourable to you and accepting it will support your fate. Initially, you had no difference of opinion with me. I've always felt honoured, as you have accepted my guidance. The bond between us has grown stronger over decades. I have never misguided you and never let you fall in trouble, so how can this prediction go wrong? Crystal is indeed a brave boy, and you are in awe of him. The matter is about his parents, which is not a big deal for you or me to settle.' Saying this, Chandaliyan gave a wicked smile, and even Chief was assured.

He clapped twice, and a man entered. He asked the man to inform Crystal's father his presence was sought by the Chief and to fetch him to the place with respect. Within a few moments, the bearded man entered the room.

'Ah...yes. Please be seated,' Chandaliyan said, offering a chair to Crystal's father.

The bearded person was about to sit on the floor beside the chair.

Chandilayan pointed to the chair again. 'You can take your seat here. I'm glad you haven't forgotten your manners or status, that is good.

Now you must get used to this upgraded status which has been bestowed upon you because of your son's fortune.'

The man sat on the chair very uncomfortably.

'From now on, you are going to be Chief's relative. We have seen your faithfulness in the past. Maybe this will be the most suitable reward for you. Your son is more influential than you were and is even stronger than you were at that young age,' Chandaliyan said.

'Where were you all these years? After the game you went missing without even accepting the reward,' Chief exclaimed.

'That day is unforgettable. Whenever I recall the events of that day it hurts me. I would be grateful if you end that discussion here,' the bearded person responded.

'The past is the past. As you know, your son is getting married to Chief's only daughter, Ritwi.'

'Pardon me, but this will not be a relationship of equals. Chief and me as in-laws, it is a dream, a dark dream, which may not be good for anyone. I'm here at my son's request; I didn't even know where he was going to bring us. If I had known I would have made him understand that we are slaves and a slave's relation with the master can be nothing but serving and being served. I will get him to understand and he will suppress his desires for your daughter. I will make him realise the truth now.' Crystal's father started moving towards the closed door.

Chief rose from his seat and shouted, 'Satrugna, wait!'

26. The Altering Affairs

The bearded man turned back with fear at the thundering command and his angvastram fell from his shoulders. He tried to catch the falling cloth but could manage only to grab the tail with his left hand.

The memories rushed at him again. In the arena when Satrugna placed his hands on Alishan's baby and the baby cried aloud, Alishan pulled the sword inside Flavius's body and cut his right hand with one strike, and he screamed with pain. In the gallery, Chief and Chandaliyan were watching the scene with a bit of satisfaction, as Flavius was lying dead in the arena.

'I lost my hand in the conflict and you never tried to help me.' Satrugna's voice was filled with agony. 'It was my wife who saved me after the conflict, and she has given me the strength to lead my life, forgetting the past. I fear the same scenario will take place with my son.'

'Satrugna...!' Chief yelled out.

'Calm down Chief, the tension in him must spill out,' Chandaliyan said to Chief.

'Satrugna, don't dig out past incidents. The future is ahead of you and your son will be crowned as the successor of the Chief. After Mathews, your son will be the next Chief of Kumbhgarh. This is the reward for your involvement in the murder of Flavius; your loss is being repaid to you with interest.'

Chandaliyan cajoled and calmed Satrugna. Now his eyes were moist with raised hopes. He seemed a different man than the one Chief had seen in the arena so many years ago.

'Aryan, where are you?'

Alishan's voice was throbbing in the lonely forest. The forest was echoing with her voice and following her, and even the tiger was calling out for Aryan. The birds and other animals were in search of Aryan. Every animal in the forest was searching for him.

Alishan was terrified as there had been no trace of her son for the past day. It felt like a decade to her.

The moment Aryan had argued with his mother was the last time she had seen his face. After that, Alishan had turned her face and left the cave to avoid Aryan's questions. She had been awaiting a bad omen as she and her son were not safe in the absence of Swami Brahmanand.

The tigress was running with Alishan, looking for any possible trace of Aryan. Even the tigress felt guilty for not having been with him when he disappeared.

The night had darkened the forest, but not a single animal had been left ignorant of the news of the missing Aryan. Just then a night-bird came flying and perched on a stone near Alishan and the tigress.

Alishan was still calling, 'Aryan...Aryan...'

The night-bird started squealing to attract attention. Alishan was not aware of the languages of other organisms, so she was helpless.

Alishan had searched the whole forest all day, not even stopping to eat. Hunger and tiredness brought a feeling of nausea and dizziness.

She moved to the stone where the bird had perched. The bird was unsuccessfully trying to find a way to communicate with her. It sat on her shoulder, clawed her *saree* and initiated flight.

This unusual activity made Alishan wonder, and she followed the bird. One end of the *saree* was in the bird's claws and the other end was wrapped around her. The bird flew low, holding one end of the *saree* to guide Alishan to the end of the forest near the sea shore. Alishan was still confused, but as soon as she approached near the sea, she tried to read meaning into the bird's gestures.

The bird left the end of her *saree* and chirping, flew towards the sea in the direction Aryan has gone when he was in the boat. This gesture of the bird brought a sense of understanding to Alishan. 'I am close to unwinding the mystery,' she thought.

'Is this about Aryan?'

The bird stopped its flight and being stable in the air, it flapped its wings.

'Where did he go?'

The bird moved in the same direction and returned.

'Did he go alone?'

The bird restlessly moved here and there.

'Was someone with him?'

The bird flapped its wings.

'Oh God!' Alishan sat down on the sand with a thump, and the wild cat came near and rubbed its face on her arm, trying to pacify her. Mourning was inevitable and uncontrollable for her. The animals from the forest shared her sorrow, standing beside her.

The big cat rushed into the water. It swam in the direction pointed out by the bird. The bird was flying just above the swimming cat. Seeing this, Alishan called out to the tiger to come back.

As soon as it came out of the water, it shook its body to dry itself. When it growled, hope rose in Alishan.

'My son will be alright; I need not panic. This is just a test and I've to stay strong enough to pursue my goal, my revenge, his revenge, our revenge… '

She convinced self, collected her strength and moved into the forest with moist eyes. The tiger looked behind for a moment towards the sea and then followed her. All the other inhabitants of the forest were now silent. Everything seemed still, with only the waves striking the shore. The sky seemed to be turning reddish.

Alishan felt an urge to meet her father. She walked towards the bamboo hut, followed by the tiger.

When she entered, she was surprised to see her old father lying down on the mud floor and shivering, trying to reach the silver water jug.

Alishan took the silver water jug and tried to make him drink. She made him sleep on her lap and started taking care of him like a child.

177

Soyumbhu Murthy was silent; tears were making their way from his eyes and reaching her hands.

'What happened, Father?' Alishan asked in a worried voice. 'I am here; your daughter is here. Nothing will happen to you...' She tried to console her father, but he was shivering and was silent. Alishan tried to press his head and hands, but in no time she found him closing his eyes. She was dumbstruck at seeing her father like this. It took a moment for her to realise that her father was no more. She cried aloud.

With the help of the tiger, she arranged the funeral of her father. After putting fire to the dead body, she sat there all alone, staring at the red sky.

By this time, Aryan and Ritwi had almost reached the centre of the land. It bore a clear resemblance to the description they had been given by the beast as well as that of the tree; the centre of the land was completely barren. Seeing the barren land, Ritwi was confused. Throughout the mysterious land, she had marked dense flora, but over here there was not a single blade of grass on the ground. Both of them were standing outside the radius. It was time for the final stage.

They did not dare to enter the last stage as they had been told that the guard would prevent anyone from entering. Their eyes were searching for signs of another person. For a long time, they moved in a circle until finally, Aryan decided to take the first step ahead. As soon as his feet touched the barren land, the ground started trembling. Ritwi started squealing as she had never experienced anything of this sort. She sat down on the ground, holding Aryan's leg.

Aryan stayed still. Soon the trembling slowed. The calm in the atmosphere was just like the peace of death, completely silent without a single movement.

Ritwi was about to stand when the land started vibrating again, but this time with less magnitude. There was a sudden landslide followed by a quake which created a ditch deep in the ground, and a tunnel. It was a deep and dark tunnel from whence strange and frightening sounds emerged. As soon as the complete tunnel came into sight, the mild vibration stilled. Aryan moved to go into the tunnel and Ritwi followed him. Ritwi, frightened by the terrible sounds from the tunnel, stepped back.

'We have to make it quick; this tunnel may close or disappear,' Aryan said.

'I don't think I can go inside. I don't have the guts to face such danger in the dark. I would prefer to wait here until you come back,' Ritwi said, unprepared to follow Aryan.

27. Inside the Deadly Tunnel!

'I won't leave you here and move in to the tunnel. What if some trouble arises after I go inside? You are not trained to face such dangers, so don't be stubborn. Just follow me,' Aryan insisted and tried to calm the frightened Ritwi.

With such inspiring and motivating words, Aryan convinced her to follow him. Aryan had won her trust quickly. They were moving deep into the tunnel, and did so as long the way was visible. But as the visibility decreased, Ritwi was troubled. Aryan led the way in the dark by holding her hand. Sometimes she got scratched by the lying stones but because of her trust in him, she continued.

A deep snore bewildered Ritwi and she stopped. This loud, fearful snore was like that of a demon. The underground tunnel was echoing with the sound. Aryan couldn't decide which path to choose from the three before him. Ritwi was not able to visualise the three ways in the dark but even then after being asked by Aryan, she chose one for them to follow. She was speechless when Aryan asked the reason for her choice, as she had no specific rationale. It was now Aryan who had to decide the path among the three.

Aryan concentrated on the smells that were emerging from the tunnels.

The awful smell was dreadful and as soon as Ritwi inhaled it, she vomited.

'Are you alright?'

'I'm feeling uneasy because of the dreadful smell.'

'Ritwi did you smell a pleasant smell as well?'

'I'm unable to, because of the awful one.'

'Concentrate on the pleasant one and close your eyes. You will feel at ease.'

Ritwi followed his advice and realised it was effective. Ritwi regained her ease and asked Aryan to move forward.

Aryan facing the three possible ways folded his hands and closed his eyes.

'Guruji, please guide me with your blessings. I'm confused, I'm not able to find the way that will lead me to success and fulfill the promise.'

Aryan felt some positive vibes rushing through his veins and nerves from his heart to his mind and all over his body. He opened his eyes with a new energy; they were glowing with enthusiasm and spirit. He moved his eyes along the three paths. Two of the three routes were well furnished and clean, but the third looked strange, with stones and thorns on the path.

Aryan put down his folded hands and caught Ritwi's left hand in his right. He moved ahead towards one of the three paths.

'Ouch…' Ritwi squealed. 'A thorn pierced my feet…'

'Have patience Ritwi. This path is the one filled with stones and thorns.'

'Why did you choose this way? This is not the right one.'

'Why do you think so?'

'The troubles at the starting point make it obvious this is not the right path, and the awful smell is getting stronger with every step. This is certainly not the right path, so why did you choose this one?'

'All that glitters is not gold. In my opinion, the right path is full of troubles and by overcoming the troubles, we can reach our destiny, and success will be on our side. Have faith in me. Maybe we can make success on this path.'

'I hope so!'

Both of them moved along the path, stepping on the stones and thorns. Their wounded feet started bleeding. Ritwi was not able to see the blood but could feel the heat of it streaming out. She bit her lower lip and joined her hands to Aryan's help her to bear the pain. Aryan could sense Ritwi was in pain, but he hardly had any option, and he struggled in the dark himself.

After moving some distance, the snores seemed to be getting intense, profound and loud. Ahead the view was astonishing; the dark tunnel opened up in a large spacious area.

There were big banyan trees and many roots hanging down, touching the ground. The area seemed lit naturally but the source of this light was not visible. It was quite astonishing to them, a secret tunnel under an entirely barren ground leading to this vast land with huge banyan trees. It was quite mysterious, impossible to believe. Ritwi vomited as the awful smell was unbearable now. With the sound of vomiting, a low pitch growl was heard that alerted both of them. They held each other's hands and moved forward. Ritwi put her other hand on her face, covering her mouth and nose. A chill wind was blowing throughout the area which enthralled both of them.

As they were moving towards the banyan trees, their legs became trapped in a marsh. The mud glued their legs to the ground in a manner which made Ritwi more afraid. The splashing from their movement created a sound which made the low growl grow stronger. Aryan gathered his strength and was able to move his trapped legs, and then he helped Ritwi and asked her to calm down.

The loud cry was now clearly audible. It was echoing all around. While trying to get Ritwi out of the trap, Aryan got distracted by a movement at the base of a huge old banyan. Patches of mud started falling from. The falling mud patches were dissolving slowly in the water.

A mud-stained man half submerged in the water started moving his hands, flaking the mud from his wrinkled skin. The man was completely drenched in the mud stains all over, and as soon as the dried mud dispatched, the hybrid termites moved up to the tree very fast. The muddy water seemed blood-mixed, and it appeared unusual. They could now see an old man whose head was settled at the tree's base. His long hair was smeared in mud, and looked like prop roots hanging from the banyan tree.

His brown eyes opened for some time and then closed again out of weakness. The nostrils started smelling something, and his neck turned towards both of them and then stopped. Now his dried black lips parted and a wicked smile played on the old and ugly face.

As the ugly mouth opened, Aryan saw two canine teeth. They looked long and sharp enough to tear raw flesh in one bite. A long tongue emerged from the cavity of the mouth licked the dried lips trying to give a moist touch.

The growl now turned into a laugh.

'Welcome. I sense you are young but you can quench my thirst.'

As guided, Aryan didn't try to mess with the old man. He had by then rescued Ritwi from the trap and moved towards the bank of the muddy stream.

The old man turned his face.

'It has been years since my throat has been filled with blood and with growing age, my ability to move has been restricted. Please come closer, as you are not visible to me.'

Aryan and Ritwi didn't have any clue as to what was going to happen to them. They moved towards the old man, but Aryan's eyes were searching for the hidden statue. The man's wicked smile broadened and the old man was growing energetic as they came nearer. The still body was moving a bit now, but his hair held him in place. Whenever he tried to move, the hair pulled him back and with the pain he growled. Hearing his growl, Ritwi was frightened. Aryan stopped.

'Why did you stop? Please come ahead, and help me to quench my thirst.'

'Friend, I have no problem with helping you. I would be glad to help you.'

'Then why did you stop?'

'You need to tell me where I can find water here so that I can bring it to you.'

The old man chuckled.

'So you think water can quench my thirst! No, it's something else that you have...'

'What's that?'

'You are here to quench my thirst. I can moisten my dry throat with your blood.'

Ritwi stepped back. She was holding Aryan's hand tightly. The old, thin and weak hand started searching for something in the muddy water. As the old man leant a bit, his long hair remained on the ground, rooting him in place. He yelled in pain.

Aryan seemed about to move to help, but Ritwi stopped him. The old man now concentrated on his hand that was deep inside the muddy water. He found something under the water which turned his cry into a smile. With great effort, he managed to bring an object out of the mud. It was a sword which was completely covered with mud and when the patches of wet mud fell down, patches of rust replaced them.

The old man managed to cut the hairs that were fixed to the ground, and then he began to sniff the air, trying to smell fresh blood. Finally, he found and caught hold of Aryan's leg.

28. Accomplishing the Promise

'Don't ever mess with the old man. If possible, try to help him.'

Aryan remembering the words of the tree, he released his hands from the tight grip of Ritwi, who moved to a safer place. The old man had held Aryan's leg and was ready to bite, but as soon as he set his teeth on his leg, instead of tearing the flesh, the canines broke and fell from his mouth.

The old man's eyes moistened and Aryan realized how eager he had been to quench his thirst. He bent down and held the old man's shoulder and tried to lift him up, but couldn't. The old man shouted, but he was unable to ignore Aryan's caring touch. Aryan didn't try to apply force.

The words of the talking trees were echoing in Aryan's ears. 'If possible help him, be polite, and avoid any arrogance.'

Aryan picked up the sword that was full of rust. He kept the big blade on his palm and brushed it. It resulted in a deep cut on his palm, which poured blood. As the blood droplets began to fall, the old man grew attentive as the smell of blood touched his nose.

The old man crawled towards Aryan, his long tongue hanging out of his mouth. The long tongue touched the blood sprinkled on the ground and greedily licked it up. Seeing this, Ritwi grew worried for Aryan. The old man took a deep sniff again. It seemed he was guiding himself by smell and touch, unable to see through his aged eyes.

Aryan lowered his hand. The old man sensing the aroma of the blood got excited and he caught hold of Aryan's hand. Aryan didn't resist and allowed the old one to quench his thirst with his blood.

After a while, the old one seemed satiated, and Aryan looked drained from the loss of blood. Ritwi was stuck in a corner, wondering how they would fulfill the conditions and get out of this place.

The old man had gained power as soon as he had quenched his thirst with Aryan's blood. The wrinkles on his face and body started to disappear, and he grew stronger. His long white hair started turning grey, and soon the old man was standing on the ground in all his glory.

Aryan lost consciousness, and seeing the old man getting stronger, Ritwi also lost her senses and fell down.

The cold breeze touched Aryan's nose, and he sneezed. He had regained consciousness. He slowly opened his eyes, and what he saw left him confused. He was on level ground, and there were no trees around. Slowly, he lifted his head and levered himself up to a sitting position. His eyes started searching for Ritwi and he saw a body lying on the earth. He rushed towards the body and found it was Ritwi. He leant down to confirm whether she was alive or dead. He laid his finger near her nose to feel her breathing, and relaxed when he realized she was still alive.

'I'm here, in front of you.'

Aryan turned around, and saw the old man who had grown stronger and younger.

'Yes, I'm the old one to whom you just gave blood. I'm impressed by your selfless attitude, and your dedication to your task.'

'Do you know why I'm here?'

'There is no other reason for a human to come to this land. Selfish humans come here to get the black magical power or pure souls come and get corrupted.'

With this description, Aryan was dumbfounded.

'How is the old man aware of who I am? Apart from physical strength, he certainly has magical powers.'

'Yes, I have the ability to read your mind as well,' the old man replied, with a smiling face.

Aryan's eyes widened, but he was distracted by Ritwi's screech. Holding her head, she sat up. She searched for him and was grateful to see him standing.

'I am impressed and overwhelmed by your passion, dedication, and purity. You are the second human I have met with such thoughts. Come closer, my boy,' the old man said.

Aryan was hesitant to move freely, and even Ritwi was struck with panic once again.

But as soon as Aryan approached him, the old man stretched his hands towards Aryan and rested them on his shoulders. Ritwi was quivering with fear, but Aryan was robust enough to face the circumstances.

'You are here to fetch the evil idol and destroy it, isn't that so? I have guarded it for millennia and faced several humans who had evil intentions. If they had acquired the idol, evil powers and desires would reach their peak, and this would have been the reason for mass destruction. The power of the dark would have engulfed this universe. I was appointed by the archangels to protect the idol from the evil minds and was expecting a pure human like you. Now you are here, and it's my time to bid farewell.'

The old man closed his eyes and muttered mantras. Behind him, an idol appeared. Winds started blowing through the forest, massive branches from trees fell for no reason and even rain started dripping, and though it was the time of sunset, the day darkened like coal. Ritwi felt terrified and rushed towards Aryan and held his hand. The old man now raised his hands towards the sky and chanted. Now the terrifying atmosphere was going back to normal. The old man opened his eyes and stepped aside for Aryan to see what he had come for.

Ritwi hid her face behind Aryan's shoulder, and Aryan closed his eyes for few moments until the old man spoke.

'This is the real face of evil, ugly, disgusting and strange. Only a wise person like you can control the evil powers from acting upon self, and you are here to demolish this threat to the universe. You are one of millions of saviours and the only one of this era. Step ahead and drown this in the deep sea as per your instructions.'

Aryan seemed a bit troubled and confused.

'Yes, you do have another responsibility; you are in search of skeletons indeed.'

'Skeletons? I...actually I don't know, but I feel something is incomplete...I don't remember, but ...'

You are under an oath, not of the present era but from an earlier life. You had promised them that they would find eternity by your grace. You had promised. Now you are here to do what you had promised. I have it secured just behind the idol. Now, execute your responsibilities.'

The old man stretched his hand, and a big piece of cloth along with other necessities like fire and holy water appeared from thin air. Aryan took them, gave the water vessel and fire to Ritwi and spread the cloth behind the idol. He collected the skeletons on the cloth and tied them up and as soon as he lifted up the idol, the old man started dissolving into the air.

'I am done with my responsibilities, and it's time to bid farewell. Be as you are lad. You have many other responsibilities to execute ahead. Remember your past and work with a pure heart. God be with you and give you strength.'

As soon as the old man disappeared, Aryan and Ritwi made their way to the shore. As they moved through the woods, the trees greeted Aryan and wished him well, even asked him to visit them again. Aryan expressed his gratitude towards them and promised to meet them again.

The breaking waves were glittering in the moonlight. Aryan opened up the cloth and threw the skeletons into the breaking waves with fire, holy water and soil. Next, Aryan tossed the evil idol in the water with a big splash.

The water erupted up like a volcano spewing lava, and in the forest, the trees started dancing and waving their long branches. Now it was time to leave! Aryan turned behind and shouted:

'I am thankful to all of you, for guiding and protecting me. I am happy that I could help someone. I promise I will be back soon and I hope this forest would be filled with wildlife within the time I once again approach here.'

Aryan helped Ritwi into the boat. As their boat set sail, Aryan caught a glimpse of the beasts, who had now shed their forms, and looked human. Aryan was happy to see it.

29. Eclipse of Yesteryear Begun Shaping

A big yajna had been arranged by Guru Chandaliyan and the villagers brought to him their livestock, thinking that if he sacrified them, they would have good fortune ahead.

'God wants you to free them from the circle of karma. You are relieving their pain and suffering and giving them the mercy that they need! As they are relieved from suffering, so you will be relieved from all your worries!'

One by one, Chandaliyan was burning the animals in the fire of the Yajna, chanting mantras. People felt assured that their bad days were gone. After sacrificing 108 live animals in the fire, he smiled. His eyes were red, and a mouth full of blood was visible. He drank the blood of those tamed animals with the help of his black magic. The villagers folded their hands and bent down at his feet, hoping that he would take all their worries away.

When they had departed, he spoke to himself.

'My twenty-one years of asceticism can't go in vain. This has been

192

everything for me, and I have loved it. For this, I have sacrificed everything: my family, my brother and today, I can sacrifice anything that comes in my way. Maybe history will remember me as a selfish man, but I am the true man. Nothing can influence me, I am self-influencing. My austerity is going to take its proper shape, and soon, I will be the demigod of all!'

A young woman came into his vision. He thought the woman had originated from the same Yajna fire. He noticed her moving through the open door. He got up from his place and walked towards the door. When he came out, he realized it was midnight, and the place was full of darkness. He was unable to see; it was a very foggy night. The only sound audible was that of the night creatures. He walked in search of the silhouette and then he heard a voice.

'It's time for you to sacrifice your own.'

'If you are trying to chase tomorrow, forget it. Tomorrow is mine. I am the demigod,' Chandaliyan shouted.

The woman appeared before him. Chandaliyan was unsure whether he was seeing a real woman in front of him or whether he was just dreaming!

He tried to touch her, and he felt her hairs fanning in the wind. Her long silver earrings were visible. From her long neck, a glittering silver chain with a rudraksha pendant hung. A blood-colored *saree* added to her elegant look. Chandaliyan tried to remember whether he had seen her somewhere before.

'Tomorrow is mine. Ages of asceticism had a disastrous sequel to our incomplete love. I am going to marry the man of my dreams, once again!'

'My soul longs for oceans of love, it longs for sands of devotion and purity and for those realms of time where our story was written years ago' a synthetic its existence visible, separating his self from behind the woman.

The man showered her with endearments and kissed her passionately. She longed to have him on her bed. Chandaliyan followed them, and they moved into his bedroom. The man reclined on it with grace, and whispered, 'You are the one my body was longing for! Don't worry, I will try to give you the best of me.'

The beauteous lady absorbed the heat that hurt her, but it was a pleasure beyond description. She consumed the warm, luscious honey aroused from his body when his penis jumped against her.

The sweet moan of love and lust disturbed Chandaliyan. Perhaps that was the couple's intent!

'Stop... I don't believe in all this nonsense. "Fuck and forget" makes sense but love is a poison; it sees no tomorrow! Love is a curse; it takes away everything.'

Both of them smiled at him. 'Your time is over, Chandaliyan. We have invaded your space, and now you have to sacrifice!'

Now instead of people, he seemed to see two serpents making love. Chandaliyan was confused and extremely disturbed. The vision was interchanging rapidly, couple changing from human to serpents and vice-versa. Sweat dripped from his forehead. The two big serpents expanded and blew venom in his face. He got scared but had no idea who they were and what they expected from him.

'The soul has got a body to rest in and now the time is near. Don't be afraid. Still, you are the demi-god. Your prediction can never go wrong. Your prediction, our curse is going to take its shape! Though it took twenty-one long years to confront you, we have no remorse as finally, we have accomplished everything...'

The eclipse of yesteryear had started taking its shape. Maybe Chandaliyan was aware of this consequence and because of his fear; his mind was conjuring these visions. Though he was being confronted with the truth, he wanted to ignore it.

But how long could the clouds of yesteryear envelope the rays of the truth? What exactly is the eclipse? Is it just a nightmare conceived only in dreams, as Chandaliyan believed? Or there is some secret to be unfolded with the sequel of an incomplete love, incomplete history that is yet to be written, marking the footsteps of those who believe in love, humanity and the Almighty! No one knew, or maybe it was all in the open, but no one could shed the natural indifference to such mystery!

To be continued...

COMING SOON
The Perplexing Curse

Rise of an eternal love...

The thrilling Sequel to

An Eclipse of Yesteryear

Ritwi was a prisoner in her own castle and guarded by two guards outside her room. As the evening approached, Crystal came to her door.

Ritwi asked Crystal to help her to move out of the castle and Crystal agreed her to help her out at midnight. Crystal helped Ritwi to move out of the castle but was with her all the time and inquired where she intended to go. Ritwi promised him that she would only visit the old temple as she did every time she felt sad, depressed and hurt.

As Ritwi entered the old temple, the same instant appeared once again!

The bells in the temple clanged. The wind lashed the trees and the villagers shut themselves inside their homes, scared.

Crystal himself was pushed away by the wind.

Ritwi was yelling 'Maa!' but her mother didn't appear in the temple instead the blurred figures appeared in the temple. The moving figures entered the main temple where the idol was placed and the purohit was chanting the sacred mantras. At the door, a lady stood with folded hands.

When the rituals of the prayer were finished the same lady called out from behind Ritwi. When she turned, she was shocked to find her mother with a young appearance.

When Seliana moved forward towards the lady, Ritwi was shocked to find the same lady with whom they had met in the dark and mysterious forest.

The Purohit was the same person Ritwi had seen standing just before her in the mysterious forest.

The Purohit and his wife stood with their hands raised for blessings and Seliana laid herself at their feet.

Everything was frozen and the light turned into darkness.

Ritwi tried to explain what had worried her.

Her mother seemed to be less worried and was expecting some other question from Ritwi but Ritwi was only worried about the past few days, her first love and the reaction of her father.

Bringing these questions to an end, Ritwi was then guided by Seliana's immortal form that helped her to understand the essence of her past connected with her present.

"Now the time has arrived when you should know the exact facts that are correlated with your past as well as your future."

Arjun had been the purohit of this temple. He was the perfect man and was supported and loved by his wife Subhadra, who was arrogant, smart and highly knowledgeable. They were considered the couple who worked on behalf of the gods to keep down evil powers. Their lives seemed to be spinning in front of Ritwi.

'I'm not interested in knowing the history of these couples. I have seen them in the mysterious forest, what is the reason behind this?'

Seliana confirmed that both of these are closely related with Ritwi in her past and her future.

Ritwi was worried about her future and her life partner. Seliana confirmed that the boy whom she had met in the forest was indeed part of her destiny.

Ritwi felt guilty for having offered him her body. Seliana smiled and helped her to travel to the times of yesteryear when the Brahmin couple was involved in love making in their cottage beside the temple. All of their interactions refreshed the memories that Ritwi had experienced with Aryan.

Ritwi was embarrassed to view the intimacy between the two couples in front of her mother. Her mother consoled her saying that it's the reality of life, and without this truth, life couldn't be sustained. This is the theme of love which is the inbuilt gift in all organisms.

Ritwi closed her eyes, sounds of young love was all that she could hear!

'Tomorrow is ours, ages of asceticism will bring a disastrous sequel to our incomplete love and I will marry the man of my dreams, once again!'

'My soul longs for the oceans of love, it longs for sands of devotion and purity and for those realms of time where our story was written years back' a synthetic its existence visible, separating his self from behind the woman.

ABOUT THE AUTHORS

DEEPAK RANJAN:

A resident of Bhubaneswar (Odisha), after pursuing his Master's degree, Deepak shifted to Bangalore to begin his career in Wipro Technology. Currently, he is working with Mindtree Ltd. He spends his leisure time doing photography, sketching, reading spiritual books, writing screenplays and creating storyboards.

Deepak's debut novel, *Nights of the Velvet*, was based on real life characters and focused on true incidents. This is his second work of fiction.

NITESH KUMAR:

Being passionately related to the art and media world, after pursuing his graduation, Nitesh picked this field as his profession. With an interest in story writing, sketching and terracotta from his childhood days, he has continued to pursue the same.

Nitesh initiated his first step independently working on his first short film followed by another short film and a documentary film. Getting confident with the executed works as a nuclear director, he stepped in the glamorous world as an Assistant Director. He directed two promotional songs for *Nights of the Velvet*. Soon after that, he spread his creativity and imagination on paper with his first work of fiction, *An Eclipse of Yesteryear*.